THE DAMNED

TALES OF THE FEISTY DRUID™ BOOK 6

CANDY CRUM

MICHAEL ANDERLE

DISRUPTIVE IMAGINATION

If we missed anyone, please let us know!

Editor
Jen McDonnell

THE DAMNED

PROLOGUE

Just outside the area of greatest impact, lying amongst the damage, were several people. Some of them were dead, their bodies mangled and blown apart, while others were unconscious, near death.

On the ground, but separate from the rest among charred grass, plants, and trees that still smoldered and cracked with the intense damage that had been done to them, laid a young woman. She didn't move, didn't breathe, and was facedown with blood pouring from her ears and down her face.

Her eyes shot open, and a deep breath painfully filled her lungs. A scream bubbled up in her chest, but her broken ribs wouldn't allow her to call out as she continued to gasp for air, tears coming to her eyes.

Slowly, she stood on shaky legs, clutching at her side as she leaned against a tree and looked around the area with blurry eyes. The light that shone through what was left of the canopy blinded her, and there was an intense ringing in her ears. Everything else sounded muffled in comparison, like she was listening through a thick pillow.

Smoke was wafting into the area, and though it wasn't enough to choke her, she certainly felt the dryness in her throat and nose with every painful breath. She could hear the faint crackles of the trees still on fire echoing through her impaired ears, and something else made its way to her.

Is that crying?

It was only a faint sound, but it seemed foreign to her right then.

Letting it go, the woman turned, taking in the sights around her. A few yards away, she saw what must have been gallons upon gallons of blood, splattered all over the trees and forest floor; intestines, organs, and human limbs littered the ground all around her. There were also intact bodies lying all over, but she didn't recognize any of them.

She felt cold inside, distant. No sadness. No anger. No emotions of any kind.

She felt as if she were asleep, dreaming. None of it was real. Not the burning forest or the mutilated bodies, however that had happened. Not the scent of smoke or death around her. Not the crying men and women on the ground that grasped at her ankles as she walked by.

It was all a dream.

Her ears still ringing and her eyes still sensitive to the light, the young woman stumbled through the woods, periodically wiping the blood streaming down her forehead. It continued to drip down her brows and into her eyes.

She came to a stop, leaning against a tree, and wondered if her body knew something that she didn't. *Am I tired? I don't feel tired...*

She sighed, letting that go, too. It didn't matter. She wasn't really in control of herself, and that was fine. It was just a dream. She would be awake soon. She continued to walk, not knowing where she was going, and not caring. She just needed to get away from that mess, that nightmare.

Before long, she came to the edge of a river. There was something familiar about it, but she just assumed it was the dream playing tricks on her. She smiled suddenly as she looked down at the rushing water.

She wondered how badly it would hurt to bend over and take off the boots she didn't remember putting on. She decided against removing them—they would dry eventually. It was the water that was important now. *Maybe it will help me wake up.*

The ringing in her ears had yet to stop, but through it, it sounded as though someone was screaming at her from below the surface of the water.

She smiled, a laugh threatening to come forth. *That can't happen. They would drown.* She shook her head and quickly wiped away the blood that dripped into her eyes, burning them unmercifully.

There it was again: the sound, that yelling. It was louder now, but she couldn't understand what that person was saying.

It's so peaceful here. Why would anyone want to scream?

The sound came again, and this time she made out the word. "Arryn!"

Turning, she looked around. She saw nothing, but the action made her feel a little dizzy, and she laughed as she stumbled over to a large rock on the riverbank.

"Arryn!" The voice had completely broken through the ringing now. She saw a man step out of the forest and come walking toward her.

Who is he? Why is he shouting at me?

"Arryn!" he said, his voice taking on a relieved tone now instead of the frantic one it had before. As she looked at him with total confusion, the relief fell from his expression, a look of worry replacing it. "Arryn?"

She laughed again, pointing at the man who seemed terribly worried about someone named 'Arryn'. "I..." She coughed, realizing the smoke had done more to her throat than she had thought. But she would wake soon—so again, it didn't matter. "I don't know who that is. You have the wrong person."

The man stared at her, his long, blonde hair blowing slightly in the breeze. He began to shake his head a bit as he stepped closer. "*You* are Arryn."

The young woman's smile fell as he began to approach her. She had no idea who he was, and he was much larger than she was. There were knives on his belt, and blood on his clothes and hands. There were even a few drops on his face.

She thought back to the dead bodies littering the area where she had awoken.

"It was you! You hurt them." The thought occurred to her to run away, but she wanted to see where this dream went.

The man's eyes flashed green, earning a gasp out of the young woman, before he said, "I'm sorry to do this, but it's for your own safety."

Dream or not, she didn't want to stick around to see what he meant by that.

She tried to move quickly, but he was much faster. Vines shot out from the ground, wrapping her from her elbows down to her ankles. They held her tight, keeping her from moving.

The man made his move then, running up and placing his hands on either side of her face. His hands were large and very warm, and something about that warmth felt familiar as it raced through her entire body.

And then everything began to change.

Suddenly, she was painfully aware that her ribs had been crushed, and she had a splitting headache. Memories flashed through her mind, the explosions in the forest.

This isn't a dream. It's not a dream at all.

Within moments, which felt like an eternity, her ribs cracked back into place, her headache dissipated, and she took her first painless breath.

"Is it you?" he asked cautiously. "Do you know where you are, what happened?"

She slowly nodded, her expression reflecting the rage that

was quickly returning along with all her other emotions, now that her broken mind had been healed. The sight of all the bodies in the forest came back to her—that hadn't been a dream, either.

They will pay for this.

Wasting no time, Arryn said, "Get me a fucking healer. I need to be at full capacity. I made a promise to Alaric, and I'm about to make good on it."

CHAPTER ONE

Two Weeks Earlier

That morning in the forest was not unlike any other. The warriors were beginning to make their way to the pit, as they did every day. The children were all stumbling out of their parents' cabins, rubbing their little eyes on their way to meet the Chieftain.

But up and ready that morning were Celine and Samuel.

She stood, staring deep into Samuel's eyes. He swallowed hard as his brows furrowed, confusion all over his face. She gave him the softest smile before taking a step forward, and then another.

"Uh," he choked out before clearing his throat. "Wh-what're ye doin'?"

Her smile broadened as she took another step closer, sauntering toward him as she closed in. She giggled, her eyes almost twinkling as they crinkled in the corners with her genuine laughter.

"Oh, you'll see," she said as she took another step forward.

Samuel obviously felt uncomfortable and had no idea how to react.

Celine placed a hand on his chest and leaned forward, her lips only a heartbeat away from his. Her nose gently brushed the tip of his, and she smiled again. "What's wrong, rearick? You act like you've never been around a woman before."

"I-I... uh..." He seemed to be at a loss for words.

Lifting her head just a little, she kissed the tip of his nose, his eyes widening as she smiled one more time. And then everything around him swirled, as he quickly found himself flat on his back with Celine straddling, holding a dagger aimed for his heart.

"Oh! That wasn't fair at all!" he said, easily throwing her off.

She laughed, quickly climbing to her feet before making her way back over to him. "Aw, now. Don't be angry. *You* were the one who got distracted! This was an excellent exercise for both of us. I proved men really are as easy to distract with sex as they seem to be, and you now know you are very susceptible to the charms of a woman. Were I an enemy, you'd be dead."

He groaned, waving her off. "Aye, ye didn't prove a thing, lass. Ain't no woman gonna come around, flirting with me. You just caught me off-guard is all."

She gave a genuine smile as she walked over and wrapped her arms around him from behind. She placed her chin on his shoulder, her cheek resting against his. He tried to hide his sharp intake of breath, but she heard it anyway.

"Well, then, I guess that makes me special," she said softly.

Samuel reached up and rested his hand gently on hers, his thumb gently stroking her knuckles. "Aye. Now, *that*, ye might just be right about."

Celine heard footsteps approaching and stepped back, realizing their training time was coming to a close. "Thanks, rearick. I happen to think you're pretty special, too."

She gave him a genuine kiss on the cheek before delivering a quick swat to his rear end. She jumped back, laughing as he spun around to look at her with a shocked expression on his face.

"Oh, lass, yer gonna pay for that," he warned.

She winked. "Promises, promises."

Samuel gave a light laugh before running directly for her, sword raised. He opted for that instead of his normal, heavy warhammer. He had been training her every morning in both hand-to-hand and weapons combat.

She got better and better all the time, but she knew most of that was because of Arryn. Arryn was much younger, but so much stronger than Celine. It inspired her to do more, and with Samuel and her niece's direction, she was improving quickly.

Celine now met Samuel head-on, raising her sword to stop his, and the loud clang of metal rang out around them. She stepped into him, shoving him back using her body weight before running at him again.

This time, she was on the offensive, forcing the rearick to defend himself as she brought the sword down over and over again. He had taught her to judge her enemies wisely. While going in with a flurry of blows was not usually a good idea, it was certainly effective on someone slower who would not be able to keep up.

In this case, Samuel's bulk and heavier weight caused him to be slower. He was forced to opt for quick, sloppy parrying as opposed to the slower, experienced movement he would use with someone twice her size.

Soon, her speed overwhelmed him, and he tripped backwards.

With a smile on her face, she stepped forward, lowering the blunted end of her practice sword to his throat. "Point to me."

He laid there, staring up at her with an expression she couldn't quite read. *Pride? Shock?*

Before she knew what was happening, he knocked her sword out of the way and jumped up, his eyes downcast as he quickly returned his practice weapon to the rack.

"Well, I think that's good enough for today." Without another word, he turned to walk away.

What the hell just happened? she wondered.

Looking over her shoulder, she saw the shadows of approaching students.

She debated whether or not she should deal with this now or later, but she could tell something was bothering him.

"Hey," she said, making her choice and running up alongside him. "What's wrong?"

He shook his head. "Nothing at all, lass. Couldn't be better. Ye did good out there taday. Soon, ye won't need me at all."

Her brows furrowed as her expression fell. "Is that what you think? Do you think I only need you because you teach me how to fight?"

He shook his head. "No, it ain't that. I just wanted ta get outta here before those damned younger students show up. Most of 'em 're all right, but some seem ta think their shit don't stink, and they need ta be taught a different kind of lesson."

She sighed, shaking her head as she stared at him. "You rearick really are a bunch of stubborn, hardheaded men. I don't have experience with the women, but I imagine they're just as bad. If you have something to say, say it. But make it fast, because those students you like so much are coming."

Samuel opened his mouth several times, as if he wanted to say something but couldn't. Finally, Celine rolled her eyes and laughed before grabbing hold of his shirt and pulling him closer, kissing him.

He gasped, but eased into her.

Just as she felt him getting comfortable, she pulled back and placed her hand on the side of his face. "Quit being such a baby."

With that, she smiled and walked away, leaving a stunned rearick in her wake.

CHAPTER TWO

Arryn sighed as she picked up weapon after weapon, inspecting the blades and the hilts. With so much training, and so many outsiders coming in and out of the Dark Forest lately, their weapons had gone to hell from overuse.

All of the training swords were warped or dented, and some were even cracked—though this wasn't of great concern, because they had blunted edges, and rounded or squared tips. Most were still useable, but it sometimes negatively affected the way the students fought.

Worse than that, both seasoned warriors and students entering into their final advanced warrior training to become part of the druid army used real swords, and they had been destroyed as well.

Between training the Cella guard, the added Arcadians as of late, the battle in Arcadia, and increasing the training schedule for the students, as well as practice for the seasoned warriors, nearly every blade in the Dark Forest had been terribly compromised in one way or another.

They needed new steel—and fast.

"I haven't seen you concentrate on something so hard since you were a little girl."

Arryn jumped at the sound of her father's voice. She turned and smiled as she saw him looking at her with affection in his expression.

She pointed at the sword she was holding. "Damn near every blade has been destroyed or impacted in some way. Dented. Warped. Bowed. Chipped. The hilts are weak on a lot of these; one wrong hit, and they could hurt someone. Not that it matters, I guess, since we can heal them. But if the sword breaks and gouges someone through the heart or the brain, well, there's not a whole lot of coming back from that."

Sighing, she threw the sword down on the ground. "We need new ones—or to reforge the ones we have."

Christopher made his way over, eyeing the weapons rack. His fingers reached forward, lightly brushing one of the battle bruised blades. "Do you have a smith here?"

Arryn shook her head. "The Chieftain said the only smith we had in any of the three villages was an old man who died in the last attack—he *and* his apprentice. From the looks of it, the smoke overwhelmed him, and his apprentice stayed to help him. He wasn't fast enough or strong enough, though, so he succumbed as well."

Christopher's expression turned sorrowful as he listened to what the dark druids had done to the people. He knew all too well just how much they could take from someone.

"What about Arcadia? Because of you, trading with the city is back on the table. From what I've heard, your friend Amelia would be more than willing to help you out," he said.

Arryn shook her head, her mouth turning up in an unamused smile. "You're right that trade is back open, or at least it will be once everything settles, but they didn't have smiths either. While I was there, I learned just how bad their situation has become."

Christopher laughed. "Without Adrien? I find that hard to believe."

Shaking her head, Arryn said, "Oh, no. The city is *much* better off without him. I just mean their economic growth came to a grinding halt when all the nobles left. All of Arcadia's money went with them, and it hurt the city quite a bit. The laborers that lived comfortably off working for the noble people had nowhere to go, and the people from the Boulevard sure as hell couldn't afford goods, so they had to go where the money was. Arcadia lost every smith they had."

"Damn…" Christopher responded.

Arryn snorted when she heard her father swear. "Yeah, so we're gonna have to get creative. I don't know where all the blacksmiths are, but if they're working for the nobles that fled the city, we probably don't want anything to do with them, anyway. As far as I can tell, that only leaves one option."

"What's that?"

As Arryn was about to answer, Cathillian and Elysia made their way into the pit. It was the middle of the day, time for everyone to take their break, get something to eat, and spend time with family. Arryn had chosen to stay behind and inspect the weapons after they heard several complaints during training.

"I only know of one blacksmith in the Valley; his name is Roger. He's just south of the mountains in the Frozen North," Arryn said.

"You're going to go all the way up there for a steelworker?" Christopher asked with some shock.

She nodded. "He's a good, honest man, and he's helped me before. I know he'd be willing to help me again. We can't use the blacksmiths in Craigston, because the rearick are a stingy bunch, and they'll want to be paid."

Cathillian snorted as he came to stand by Arryn. "I don't know the full conversation here, but if you're discussing finding a blacksmith in the Heights who's willing to take less than a shit ton of money, you'd be better off trying to put a dress and one of those hideous little hats that the noblewomen in Arcadia wear on a lion."

Arryn looked at him incredulously. "Uh, we *could* do that. You *do* remember we're druids, right?"

He looked dumbstruck for a moment as he looked up, thinking over his comment. He laughed. "Oh, yeah. Nevermind. Carry on."

Arryn rolled her eyes and shook her head. "Anyway, as I was saying... Roger is a good man, and I know he'd be willing to work with us for little coin. He's extremely fast, too. The only problem is getting up there."

"And how far is 'up there,' exactly?" Elysia asked.

Arryn paused as she sighed. She knew Elysia would not be fond of her leaving, especially going that far away. "Like I said, just south of the Frozen North. I found him when I came down from the mountain. He's the one that crafted the ram's horn daggers for me; he did it in just a couple of hours, while I slept."

"Well, I know you're strong and more than capable of taking care of yourself, but I would still feel better if you took someone with you," Christopher said.

Elysia nodded. "If you truly feel this is the answer, then by all means, do it. I don't know how long we have, but I do know Alaric and Jerick are probably still recuperating, and they're more than likely going to need to find more people if Alaric wants to take another crack at the Dark Forest—and I have no question in my mind about that. He *will*. That buys you a week or so, I'd imagine. Maybe more, but I wouldn't risk it."

"I'll go," Cathillian said. "We've been adventuring together anyway, and even though you're stronger than most people here, it still wouldn't hurt to have someone else with you. If you'll have me, I'd gladly accompany you. Besides, you'll need the extra hands to carry back whatever this guy can make."

Arryn smiled. "Good! Then it's settled. We'll go north. Maybe we can even talk Roger into coming here, and taking an apprentice after the war is over. Obviously, we need it."

Elysia smiled. "One miracle at a time, child."

Nodding, Arryn said, "Great! We'll set out tonight. Cathillian, you and I should break away from training for the rest of the day and get some sleep. I need to tell Snow we'll be leaving. You should ready Maia."

"Take Chaos," Elysia suggested. "He's very large, and can carry a cart much faster than Maia could. You'll need it for whatever weapons you can craft. Arryn, with your magic, you should be able to create the steel for him, as you did with your blades. That way, he won't use as much magic, and will get more done."

"Do you need me to go with you?" Christopher asked. "I feel like I should, but at the same time, I realize you're not a little girl anymore."

She made her way over to her father and wrapped her arms around his neck, pulling him into a hug. "Right now, I want you to relax and continue on your healing path with the Chieftain, Elysia, and Zoe. You don't have much longer with Zoe since she'll be returning to the Heights soon. Take whatever help you can get. I'll be fine. I'll see you when I return."

Arryn gave him a quick kiss on the cheek before stepping away and heading back toward the southern village.

Taking a deep breath, Amelia walked into her new classroom. It was the first time in a very long time she had been inside the Academy. She had even avoided it during the remodel of Marie's new office.

Things were different now, and she intended to be there every step of the way this time.

In the short time that she had been back in control, Amelia had gone to great lengths to make the city stronger, and that included the Academy. The school's rules, curriculum, and even the hours of operation had been changed.

Arcadia would never again be so easy a target. It would take one hell of an effort to get the best of them in the future. Starting immediately, Amelia had begun mandatory classes in the mystical arts for *all* students.

She was more than aware that she wasn't a master of that particular branch of magic, but she knew enough to teach them how to meditate, and create a basic mental barrier—which was sorely needed.

She wanted to teach them how to shield their minds so that what happened with Scarlett and the other dark mystics could never happen again.

Of course, that would mean that not even *she* could get in their heads without their knowledge, but she didn't mind that in the grand scheme of things. Her intuition had grown significantly, and if she felt someone was in danger, she would be able to get the information she needed.

On top of educating them in the mystic arts, she had begun holding weapons classes in the larger rooms downstairs. Students would all be expected to take a basic self-defense course, which would include working with regular weapons, as well as magitech rifles. They would be training with experienced fighters.

Though the Guard wasn't as strong as they needed to be for the position they held, they were certainly strong enough to teach students basic self-defense.

Additionally, the school would no longer be open only to teenagers. Once regular classes were out for the day, the adult classes would begin.

This newest change was made especially for those who lived in the Boulevard, who hadn't had any opportunity to learn magic. They would also have the chance to learn self-defense—or continue their education, as many of them had learned how to fight in some fashion in the original Battle for Arcadia, when Hannah, the Founder, and the others had taught them.

They would have the opportunity to learn mental shielding, physical magic, and hand-to-hand combat, as well as weapons handling. Everything the younger students had the opportunity to learn in the daytime, the adults would be able to learn in the evening.

The idea was that each student would then have someone to practice with at home, or someone to help, if they were further ahead in their own classes.

Amelia's greatest hope was to have a few Cella guards training the defense classes, and maybe even have an advanced class. She had learned a lot from the druid culture, and she decided that she wanted to implement some of their practices. It had made them strong and respected.

She also wanted to talk with the Chieftain to see if he might know of a druid who would be interested in teaching a nature magic class. She had so loved the idea when Arryn first came to the city, and she still loved it now.

The city would be much safer if everyone in it knew how to fight, how to throw a fireball, how to block their minds from being assaulted, and how to heal themselves if the worst were to happen.

Amelia didn't care about power; she didn't care about being in control of the city. She only cared that she led them down the right path, the path Ezekiel had originally wanted for them.

If she had her way, Julianne would soon be making a monthly trip to the city to teach the mystical arts class, and she would have another druid in the Academy at all times. The Valley would then be a peaceful place, with all three branches of magic finally united, as well as its people.

Just the way it always should have been.

Amelia smiled as everyone took their seats and got comfortable. There were several familiar faces from when she had been the Dean, but there were many more who were from the Boulevard.

"Good morning, class," Amelia said. "I know this will be difficult for you, trying to get back into studying and learning with everything that has happened recently. But we have to move on. More than that, we have to make ourselves stronger, so that we have the *confidence* to move forward. "

The students seemed uncomfortable being back in class, and she couldn't blame them. But even though she understood, she knew it was a necessity.

It was the first day, so she took her time explaining the changes that were coming, and those that had already taken place. Though classes had resumed, there was a leniency for those who were still having a difficult time.

It would also take some time to get the word out to the adults. There were some who knew classes would be available, but most did not; that was the reason behind informing the younger students.

They were to tell their parents, aunts, uncles—whoever they might have in their lives—that the Academy was now open to everyone, and that they didn't need to worry about payment right then.

She planned to find a way to supplement the lack of income for the poor students somehow, making it free or low-cost to them. The teachers needed to be paid, but self-defense was priceless. Every student deserved to learn, no matter the amount of money their family had.

"What about Arryn? Can't she come back and teach another nature magic class? From what I heard, she was a badass in combat as well," one of the students inquired.

Amelia smiled. "I'm sure she will one of these days, but right now, she's trying to save the Dark Forest from being overtaken. Like we have seen in our own struggles recently, the Dark Forest has its enemies."

At the mention of Arryn, several of the students wore guilty looks on their faces. She had no doubt it was due to the memory of how they had all treated her. They had been so quick to point a finger at the outsider, even though she had gone to great lengths to help them. Their actions had pushed her out of the city, allowing both Talia and Scarlett to rise to power.

If it hadn't been for Arryn risking her life to come back, the city would have fallen a *few* times.

Amelia clapped her hands, rubbing them together as she smiled. "So, who wants to make sure no psycho bitch ever gets in their head again?"

Everyone in the room raised their hand with enthusiasm.

CHAPTER THREE

It seemed like it had been forever since Ren and Sven were last in Craigston, and they were flooded with relief when they made it home from Arcadia.

Amelia had gotten what she needed, having taken down a large group of bastard bandits. She even kept a live one to take back and question about what the hell was going on with all the attacks.

The two rearick men had just made it to Ophelia's, the local bar and inn located in their home town. They walked in and were cheered for immediately.

"Ta the two rat bastards responsible fer getting Arcadia ta do somethin' about the shits on the road!" someone shouted.

"Hear, hear!" everyone else shouted after.

It seemed there was a lot to celebrate.

Julianne, the Master Mystic in the Temple, had recently returned, causing quite the stir. A few weeks before, a false Julianne—a dark mystic named Donna, who had changed her appearance and posed as the Master—had come through and caused a mess.

By the time the *real* Julianne arrived, Craigston and the

Temple had been on the verge of war. Luckily, she was able to pull everything back together and set it straight; even ol' Tavich was able to help, surprisingly enough.

The rearick brothers were happy they had missed all of *that* excitement.

A barmaid came over and sat a mug of ale down on the table before each of them, giving them a wink. "The lady o' the house says these're on her. With both of ye helpin' catch those rotten thieves, more money'll be pourin' in her way."

The brothers smiled and lifted their drinks in thanks before tipping them back and draining them. Each man had a stream of ale dripping down his long beard.

Ren set his mug down first, letting out a large belch and wiping his mouth with the back of his arm. His brother followed shortly after. "Thanks, lass," Ren said to the barmaid. She nodded, picking up both mugs before turning and heading back to the bar.

"I think we might just be able ta get used ta this whole town hero thing," Sven said.

Ren laughed. "I did this in Arcadia fer a bit after helpin' with the remnant. Trust me, they get used to it after a while, an' the free drinks quit comin'. Enjoy it while it lasts."

The barmaid had just set down their new drinks when the town alarm began to sound. Everyone in the bar turned serious, even those that were obviously piss drunk.

Ren and Sven jumped up, hustling out the door to see a young rearick with a short beard running toward them. It was Gabe, the one in charge of the watchtower.

The young lad began pointing toward the east, trying to gain his breath. "Th-they're... comin'. From the... east. Remnant. Lots of 'em."

The brothers looked to one another before nodding. Ren turned back to the young man and put his hand on his shoulder.

"If ye're brave enough ta fight, grab a hammer. If not, get yer ass inside the bar."

He could see the debate in the young man's face before he finally ran toward the bar.

"What a little runt," Sven said. "When I was his age, I was fightin' remnant in me sleep!"

Ren laughed. "Yeah, that's 'cause ye were asleep whenever I was fightin' 'em. I'd rather the boy know he can't fight and run inside, than pretend 'e *can*, and us have ta save his ass eighteen times before gettin' me-own-self killed."

Sven nodded. "Aye. Good point."

The men ran inside, grabbed their weapons, and shouted to the drunkards, miners, laborers, and anyone else inside that the town needed defending. When they all piled outside, they saw several armed women running out into the open.

More and more, this was becoming the norm for the small town. Not that they minded, especially after seeing what the women in Arcadia could do.

Ren could hear the sound of growling and screaming as the remnant tore their way into town. "Move east! We don't want these bastards takin' our bar!"

Sven stepped forward. "Yeah! We won't have anywhere ta drink afterward ta celebrate rippin' their heads off!"

The men and women ran forward, searching in the darkness to find the beasts that were coming to attack their home. Ren couldn't help but think of just how far from home those half-rotted maggots were.

He imagined it had less to do with their willingness to travel, and more to do with the fact that Arcadia had been a massive failure. They knew moving into the Valley again would mean terrible things for them.

The first remnant came into view, jumping out with a hideous glisten to his skin, the rotted pustules and sweat and oil all over him almost shining in the moonlight. Before Ren could get to him, one of his female counterparts ran forward.

She had the war cry of a man twice her size as she swung a hammer as big as his own, smashing the beast in the side of the head and splitting it open. She spun around, dropping to her knees as she did. Her hammer came around and hit another in the side as he charged her. The beast was knocked off balance, giving her enough time to stand and bring that hammer down on the back of its neck.

Ren smiled. Their women had always been feisty and rather terrifying, but they weren't fighters. Craigston was a very patriarchal and old-fashioned community. Now, he was painfully aware of the opportunity their people had been missing out on the whole time by not including them.

The same fear the wives put into their husbands, was now being put toward taking down the monsters that threatened them.

The brothers ran forward, yelling out as they swung their hammers, taking down two remnant that charged for them. "Stick together!" Sven ordered.

Ren had no plans to do anything else. They were stronger together, and fought better as well.

Sven ran forward, striking one remnant in the side before turning and swinging upward at an angle to hit another in the face that had been approaching from behind. Returning to his previous enemy, he swung downward, snapping his leg before raising his hammer over his head and smashing the monster's skull.

The remnant fell to the ground, his head broken apart like a cracked egg.

Wave after wave came after them, the beasts having been broken up by the tree line. There were too many trees, and it forced the remnant into a staggering formation that allowed the rearick to run in and take them out, far easier than if they were out in the open.

Long ago, before Arcadia had been fully built and the Valley had become a prosperous area for farmland and noblemen, the remnant had enjoyed attacking Craigston.

It was nothing to the townspeople for the alarm to be sounded in the middle of the night, or in the middle of the day. The remnant never seemed to be far. But the rearick held strong. They refused to move and refused to give up their homeland, which resulted in the rearick people evolving.

Many believed it had been the mining life that gave the rearick their signature short, stocky build. They weren't wrong. That in combination with constantly battling the remnant caused them to be shorter, packing far more muscle into a smaller package.

Their stature was what had allowed them to survive the cold, bitter winter months, the deep and dangerous mines, and the incessant remnant incursions.

Many in Arcadia found their appearance to be amusing, but in a fight against those diseased beasts from the Madlands, the rearick stood a better chance than anyone.

The beasts didn't seem to be used to the chill in the air that came with living in the mountains, and the lower temperatures, along with the recent snow, now slowed the remnant down, making them easy targets.

"They're running!" one of the women warriors shouted out. "We ran them off!"

Not just yet, they hadn't. Ren ran forward and smashed a remnant in the belly, as his brother delivered the final blow to one that had gotten stuck in the middle of a large group of rearick.

Two female warriors wandered up, their bloody weapons slung over their shoulders as if they were on a casual Sunday stroll. One of them looked over to Ren and winked. "Nice form, old man. What else ye got?"

She smiled in a way that told Ren she meant that in a flirtatious manner. "I ain't *that* old."

She laughed. "Good. Then ye won't mind buyin' me a drink. I feel like celebratin'. If yer not headin' ta bed, there, grandpa, I'll celebrate with ye."

Ren looked to his brother, who had a rather shocked expression on his face. "I don't look *that* old, do I? I mean, hell, she can't be much younger than me."

Sven shook his head, his lips still slightly parted. "Is it me, or did 'r women get ballsier while we were gone?"

"Is that a yes? Or do I need ta club ye an' drag ye back ta Ophelia's ta get yer attention?" the woman asked.

Ren nodded. "Definitely ballsier. And, I dunno about you, but I like it. Looks like tanight is gonna turn out all right, brother. Have fun drinkin' alone."

The woman laughed as Ren made his way over. "Tanight better be better than *all right*, 'r ye'll be feeling the business end of me hammer in the mornin'."

Shaking his head, Ren said, "Oh, don't you worry about that. I don't intend on feelin' either end of yer hammer. I assume in yer hands, both ends would be the business end."

The woman threw her head back in laughter, clapping Ren on the back. "Ye'd certainly be right about that."

CHAPTER FOUR

After everything that had happened in the southern part of the Dark Forest, Corrine found herself desperate to dive deeper into anything and everything that was pure and natural among the druids.

Growing up, she had always been painfully aware of just how cruel people could be, but she had never seen the level of darkness they were capable of until Jerick was ready to end her life—the life of a child.

On top of that, she had seen the intense damage that had been done to Arryn's father, Christopher, over the course of a decade at Alaric's hands, and she would do absolutely anything possible to distance herself from her dark heritage.

Christopher had been with the dark druids longer than she had been alive. Knowing the torture that she had faced at their hands while being considered an outsider, she couldn't imagine what he had been through as an Arcadian—a *true* outsider.

All those factors combined with her own weakness as a child had been motivators for her to take her warrior training more seriously. That had been a casual decision, but she hadn't felt truly broken and desperate to be stronger and more useful until she had looked into Arryn's eyes at the moment when the experienced warrior realized that three people she cared for were about to die and nothing could be done.

In that moment, Corrine had never felt such strength, and she knew it was because of Arryn, because of everything Arryn had taught her.

Corrine never wanted to be that weak again.

In all her training sessions, she had stood with children younger than her who were so inexperienced, they weren't even allowed to spar with one another. They were just learning how to throw a punch. It was embarrassing to her because the students her age were so far advanced in comparison, she would have taken a brutal beating if she tried to start alongside them.

She didn't want to be at that low level anymore. Not after what she had seen. Life was scary outside the barrier of the Dark Forest; even inside, bad things could happen if the wrong people were motivated enough. She wanted to be prepared.

Nearly losing her life had traumatized her, but it had also driven her forward. She wanted to be more than *just a warrior*— she wanted to be one of the *best* warriors the Dark Forest had ever seen. Just like Arryn, the woman she was coming to think of as her adoptive mother.

"Are you sure you're ready for this?" Christopher asked as he accompanied Corrine to the training pit. "I've not been here long, but from what I've learned, you're about to be in a world of pain. You're so young; there's still plenty of time for this, you know." He smiled at her, resting a gentle hand on her shoulder.

She shook her head. "When I was on my knees, and the man I used to call my Chieftain had a knife raised above me, that was supposed be my final moment. I should've died. But I didn't. Who's to say something like that won't come around again?"

Christopher sighed as he shook his head, his hands clasped in front of him as they walked. "That sounds very mature. You remind me a lot of Arryn when she was little; she was mature for her age, too. I understand why you want to do this, and I admire it. I imagine I would've made this trip a thousand times with Arryn, if I'd found my way back to the Dark Forest instead of being captured in Arcadia."

There was a brief pause before Corrine responded.

"You missed a lot, but it made Arryn strong. I probably sound older than I am because I've had to survive alone and take care of myself almost since I was old enough to run. I'm a strong kid because of the way I lived before. She's a strong grownup for the same reason."

He nodded, the look on his face content. "I suppose if things had been different, Arryn would be like any other noblewoman. She would have proper manners, be courted by a young man that probably wouldn't even be *close* to being good enough for her. She would have learned magic, but I think she would've been more like me. She wouldn't have been as talented as her mom was—Arryn had no real motivation to push her through her attention deficit issues."

Corrine shrugged. "I was stuck in my magic, too. I had a hard time learning how to heal… though, I guess I haven't been here very long. Fear and anger are good motivators, just like Arryn said. I was scared of the classes for the kids my age, but I started in the *baby* classes where they told me to. I learned the basics, but I was still scared. Then everything happened."

"I'm guessing that changed your mind a bit?" he asked.

She nodded. "I learned what *real* fear was. Taking a punch from a kid my age and size isn't nearly as scary as a grownup your size holding a knife to my throat. Now, I'm not scared to test my limits. Besides, they'll heal me. The pain is only temporary."

"You're very strong. I think you'll do amazing things in those classes." Christopher smiled as he reached over and brushed her cheek with his hand. "Speaking of healing, have you seen yourself lately?"

She shook her head, her dark curls bouncing.

"When I first saw you, your skin was grey, though it wasn't quite as dark grey as Alaric's or Aeris'. Your hair suffered as well. Since we've been back, your skin has developed a beautiful brown tone and looks very healthy, and your hair has turned solid black and shines in the sun."

The girl smiled as she reached up, her hands brushing against her hair. "Really?" She pulled her hands away and looked at her skin.

He nodded. "Mmhmm. You look beautiful. More importantly, you look *healthy*. I suspect your skin and hair will continue to change. You have beautiful dark skin and hair, and beautiful green eyes. I no longer see hints of grey in them; they are a rich emerald color."

Her face lit up as she touched her cheeks. "It must have happened when I healed Arryn. Maybe it healed me, too!"

He laughed. "I think you might be right. This is a sign for you to keep moving forward. You were never anything like them, and now every trace of the connection you once had is disappearing. You have the opportunity to live a healthy, happy life that you can be proud of. I happen to think you're on the right track with this training stuff—even if I think it's a little rough. Your culture here is much different than where I'm from."

"You really think so? You think I'm ready?" she asked as they reached the pit.

Nodding, Christopher said, "I think your passion to do the right thing, the love for and from everyone around you, and your curiosity will make your dreams come true. You will undoubtedly be one of the best warriors in the entire tribe."

Rushing forward, Corrine wrapped her arms around his waist. He smiled as he reached down to brush her hair out of her face and pat her on the back.

"Thank you!" she said.

Corrine turned and ran over to Cassondra, who'd come out to

greet them and now gave Corrine a warm hug as well. Corrine turned and waved, and Christopher waved back before leaving the pit.

There were days when he could stay and watch, but other days it affected him in dark ways, triggering memories from his time with the dark druids.

"Are you ready for your first real day?" Cassondra asked Corrine when Christopher had gone.

Corrine beamed as she nodded with enthusiasm. "Yes! I think I've learned enough in the basics class with Ryel to defend myself."

Cassondra led her through the rules, preparing her as best as she could. She called Jacqueline, another student, forward.

"Jacqueline is the closest to you in experience that we have, without you going back into the younger class. That being said, she's still two years older than you. Real training doesn't usually begin until kids reach ten, and the really rough stuff comes a couple years later. Are you sure you're ready? She's been at this for several months, so when she hits, she hits hard."

Corrine didn't hesitate. "I want to get really good as fast as I can. I can't do that if I'm being babied. I know I'm still a kid, but I want to at least *try*. If I can't handle it, I'll go back to the other class."

Cassondra nodded. "Very well, then. We let our kids here make decisions for themselves when it comes to their training. If you think you're ready, you're ready. It isn't for us to decide what your limitations are. But if you decide otherwise, that's fine, too. Please know there is no shame in changing your mind. It happens often—though we don't usually let kids skip so far ahead as you."

Corrine stepped into the pit, and Jacqueline followed close behind. The older girl was only a little taller than Corrine, but her body seemed to tower over her with the lean muscle she had already developed.

Corrine took a deep breath as she and Jacqueline saluted one another.

"Begin!" Cassondra called out.

Only having experience in movement and not in actual fighting, Corrine ran forward, throwing her fist out in an attempt to punch the other girl. Jacqueline hadn't had much more experience than Corrine, but it was enough that she was able to easily dodge the blow, stepping to the side and punching hard.

Her fist connected with Corrine's nose with impressive strength. The smaller girl cried out as she felt her nose crunch, and blood immediately poured out over her mouth and down her chin.

In a flash, Jacqueline knocked Corinne's feet out from under her, taking her down to the ground with one hand on her throat. "Even with a punch to the face, never let your guard down," Jacqueline said.

"Are you giving up?" Cassondra asked in a stern tone.

Corrine tilted her head to the side, spitting a mouthful of blood out onto the ground. "Never!" she shouted back, doing her best to fight the tears that were welling in her eyes.

She had never felt pain like that, so she wasn't exactly sure how to process it, but she was grateful. Every punch she took from another student—especially one like Jacqueline, who obviously wanted to help teach her—was a punch she wouldn't have to take from full-grown man or woman who planned to kill her.

"Good girl!" Cassondra called out. "Get up."

Jacqueline's eyes flashed brighter green for a moment as heat flooded through Corrine. The injured girl closed her eyes and ground her teeth as the bones set back in place.

"Don't give up. I'll help you get better. The pain is temporary, but death is permanent," Jacqueline said as she stood, extending her hand out to Corrine.

The girls split apart by several feet, each one of them taking a defensive position. Cassondra once again announced the start of the round, and Corrine held her place. If nothing else, she had learned a lesson about rushing in, and also underestimating her opponent.

This time, Jacqueline ran forward, and Corrine spun out of the way. Jacqueline was quick, dropping down and attempting to sweep Corrine's feet out from under her again, but Corrine was ready.

Corrine jumped, and Jacqueline's leg swept under her elevated feet. When she landed, she took advantage of Jacqueline's turned back. As the older girl began to stand, Corrine rushed forward, dropped to her knees, and wrapped her right arm around Jacqueline's neck to pull her down and hold her. Corrine's left arm stabilized the hold, making it almost impossible for her opponent to breathe.

It was a move that Ryel had taught her to use to silence an enemy if she were ever able to sneak up behind them. He told her it would cut off the airflow and put her opponent to sleep, if she held on long enough.

As Jacqueline reached back to grab her, Corrine used her weight and fell back, landing flat before rolling over and forcing Jacqueline on her stomach as she continued to hold her down. As children in the younger training courses, Jacqueline had the ability to tap out if she felt the need to, and she did so now.

"Very good!" Cassondra said with a smile on her face.

Corrine followed her lead, smiling as she let go of Jacqueline and took her weight off. As Jacqueline had done for her, Corrine extended her hand to help the other girl into a sitting position. To her surprise, her opponent was smiling as she struggled to catch her breath.

"Nice job! I thought I would be able to get away from you, but I couldn't. You have quite the death grip!"

Giving a restless laugh, Corrine said, "Thank you! That means a lot coming from you."

"Everyone on your feet," Cassondra said. "Time to go again.

This is only your first day of training, so there are no winners. Tomorrow, however, will be another story." The warrior held an almost wicked smile as she winked in the girls' direction.

Jacqueline tapped Corrine on the shoulder. "Everyone thinks Nika and Elysia are the scariest, but just you wait until you see *her* fight. She's scary, too."

Corrine knew she had meant it as a warning, but after what she had seen with Arryn, deep down she felt like no one could compare to that—except maybe the Chieftain. Still, hearing just how strong Cassondra was didn't make her feel threatened; it made her feel excited.

She couldn't wait to be strong like them.

NATHANIEL SET HIS BAGS DOWN, taking one last look to make sure he had everything he needed. Today he was finally headed for Arcadia. He would be joining the Academy, and his father couldn't be prouder.

"I still feel strange, leaving when the city is just getting back on its feet," Nathaniel said.

His father, the governor of Cella, waved him off. "Don't worry about all that. Our laborers are returning soon; a lot of them already have. When that happens, Arcadia will send their laborers here just as we did for them. We have a great position with the Arcadians. I think the Valley will prosper with Amelia at the helm. Now the Temple, the Dark Forest, and Arcadia, as well as Cella, are all united for the first time. If there was ever a time for you to go to Arcadia, it's now."

"More guards are supposed to show up, though, right?" Nathaniel asked.

The governor laughed. "You're worrying far more than even I am. And yes, more guards will show. We've finished training the first group she sent us. They helped rebuild some things and gave us the added numbers in case anything happened. In return, we're sending them back trained up and ready to go. The new recruits will be here later tonight or early tomorrow, so you have nothing to worry about."

Nathaniel sighed, nodding as he lifted his bags. "Sorry. This just makes me nervous. I know the deal between Cella and Arcadia is good, but it doesn't make me worry any less about our people. You giving up experienced guards and taking on a bunch of inexperienced men and women while I'm gone doesn't sit well with me."

His father clapped him on the back, turning him gently toward the door as he escorted him out. "Then I guess it's a good thing you won't have to be here for it, right? Go. Learn. Enjoy yourself… make the best out of the situation. I'll send letters, and if anything happens, I'll send a rider out immediately. Okay?"

Nathaniel nodded, stepping forward and wrapping his father in a hug. "Take care of yourself. Don't be stubborn."

The governor smiled and helped load Nathaniel's bags into the carriage. "You do the same. On both accounts. Have fun and learn something good. Help Amelia when you can."

Nathaniel nodded once, looking around the city one last time before climbing into the carriage. The governor closed the door and waved to the driver.

As the carriage took off, Nathaniel found himself both excited and nervous about the future. He knew little about magic, but there was so much more for him to learn. And after all they had been through, he planned to bring everything he learned back to the city, to help teach them, as well.

CHAPTER FIVE

Deciding to leave the forest when everything seemed so vulnerable was a big decision, but even with an impending battle, the Chieftain, Elysia, Cathillian, and Arryn all decided it was well worth the risk. They needed new weapons, or they wouldn't stand a chance.

Their battle would not and could not be fought entirely with magic. Both sides would be exhausted if they relied too heavily on it, and it was possible no outcome but a stalemate would come from engaging in such a battle.

They needed to be prepared for anything that might happen, and going in with torn up equipment was not the way to do it.

Arryn and Cathillian had decided to go out on their own, not wanting to risk taking anyone else with them. They each felt confident they would be safe in their travels, as the bandits were primarily south, and there wasn't much up north, except for Cella.

After a day of traveling, they came across a cabin big enough to hold a large family.

"I smell cattle. We should stop and see if they will allow Snow and Chaos to drink," Arryn said.

Cathillian nodded. "Maybe we could grow something for them in return. In your experience, are people in the Valley very hospitable?"

"Surprisingly, yes. However, there were ass loads of snobby nobles that left the city when Adrien was killed, so the place might be owned by one of them. Who knows?"

"Hey," Cathillian said with a confused, yet intrigued tone to his voice. "Total change of subject, but did you get a good look at Dante before we left?"

Arryn looked at him with wide eyes, nodding. "I don't know what the hell has happened to him in the last week, but since the last attack, when he was stuck up in a tree, shaking and scared, he has been growing like a weed. He's grown over a foot since then. When we were in the mountains, he grew very quickly the first couple days, and then stopped completely. He hasn't grown an inch since, and even a normal tiger cub would have grown in the last couple months. Not a ton, but certainly a few inches, I would think."

"Yeah, I figured Dante would come into it, but he never did. I just assumed your magic had caused Snow to grow exponentially, but had somehow stunted Dante and kept him the same size. Do you really think it's everything that happened with you and Corrine?" Cathillian asked.

Arryn sighed. "Honestly, I don't see how it could be anything else. He was petrified and stuck in a tree during all that. Corrine damn near died—a couple of times—and so did I. He was tiny, and unable to do anything about it, and I know he felt my emotions. He probably even saw what I saw."

She shook her head. "I think about how terrifying that must have been for him. There is no one more important to him than his mama and me and, to a lesser extent, Corrine. Corrine and I were both in danger, and he was too little to do anything. I know the animals don't have magic of their own, but something definitely happened. Regardless, if it keeps up, he's going to be huge.

The good thing is we won't have to worry about him so much anymore."

Cathillian laughed. "*And* we won't have to pull him out of trees anymore."

Arryn groaned as she rolled her eyes. "Thank the Bitch for that."

They quieted as they rode closer to the house. It seemed rather quiet, which was either a good thing, or a very bad thing. They decided to be cautious.

Arryn climbed off Snow's back and slowly made her way to the door. She had one hand behind her back, wrapped around the ram's horn handle of her dagger, in case she was met with danger. With her free hand, she reached out and knocked.

Several moments passed before the door opened just a crack. "Who the hell are you, and what the hell do you want?"

Arryn was taken aback by the harshness in the woman's voice, but she blew it off, opting for a smile as genuine as she could manage. "Hi, my name is Arryn, and that back there is my traveling companion, Cathillian. We wanted to see if it was possible to let our animals have fresh water before we continued farther north."

The old woman eyed her suspiciously for a few moments. "That hand you have hidden… What exactly do you plan to do with it? What are you hiding?"

Arryn held her smile. "It's a dagger. No offense, ma'am, but I've met my fair share of assholes on the road. I wasn't about to knock on the door without preparing for the worst. Now, it is in fact *your* door, and I *am* a stranger, so I can't blame you for anything you might be hiding, but I didn't come here to fight. I only came for water. So, I'll take my hand away from my daggers as soon as I know I'm not gonna get one shoved in my chest."

Arryn saw the woman's body jerk with a small laugh as a wry smile spread across her lips. The door opened fully, and Arryn saw a sword at the woman's side.

"I appreciate honesty," the old woman said. "Seems to be in short supply around here these days. Now, I'm gonna put my sword against the wall over here, and I expect you to remove your hand from that blade. Do we understand each other?"

Arryn nodded. "Yes, ma'am."

As promised, the woman put her sword aside, and Arryn moved to a more natural, non-threatening position. The woman stepped outside and closed the door behind her. As she looked around Arryn, her eyes widened.

"I don't mean to point out the obvious, but are you aware there is a tiger standing back there that's damn near the size of the black Shire horse it's standin' next to?" She got a better look at Chaos, and her surprise renewed. "Bitch and Bastard... That damn horse is several hands oversized, too!"

Arryn laughed. "The tiger is Snow. She's my familiar. The horse is named Chaos, and he belongs to Cathillian's mother—also a familiar. That's why they're larger than normal."

The woman once again looked at her with curiosity and then looked to Cathillian. "Pointed ears. Familiars. Both of you are druids, yes?"

Arryn looked back to Cathillian for a moment before turning back to the old woman and giving a nod. "Yes, ma'am. Well, I was born in Arcadia, so I don't have the pointed ears, but he does. And just between the two of us, he uses those to listen in on anything and everything." She leaned in a bit and whispered, "He's nosy, and he likes to think it's funny."

"Hey! Not fair! We just met her, and you're already making me look like the bad guy here."

With a knowing smile, the old woman turned to him and said, "I have a feeling you don't need her for that."

Cathillian gave the old woman his famous fictitious offended expression. "My goodness. Fast friends, I see."

The old woman turned again to Arryn. Her hand was quick as she reached out to flip Arryn's long, dark hair behind her shoulders. "And you might've been born an Arcadian, but there's a slight point to those ears of yours. I saw just a flash of them when you turned to look at your friend earlier."

Arryn's brows creased as her fingers darted up, feeling along the top edge of her ear. It was very slight, but her ears had begun to change.

Her eyes widened. She had seen more and more emotional change in herself as of late, but this was a physical manifestation of how far she had come and how much she had changed.

The first druids to settle in the Dark Forest had seen the small changes in their ears after a few years. Like the rearick in the mountains, it was their way of adapting to their environment brought on by the nanocytes in the blood.

Each generation since, the feature had become more and more pronounced—like Cathillian's. It was hard to say just how long hers had been in the process of changing, but she certainly hadn't noticed until then, and neither had anyone else.

Though, they were almost always too busy planning war to notice such subtle changes.

The old woman nodded toward the back of the house. "Follow me. This way. The name's Elsie."

Cathillian dismounted and urged Chaos to follow him with little effort. Snow was already by Arryn's side, sticking close in case of an emergency. As they rounded the back of house, she saw several young men rebuilding a broken fence. It didn't seem to have been broken by natural means; something seemed off to Arryn.

"What happened here?" Arryn asked.

The woman gave a sarcastic chuckle as she shook her head. "What happened here? Well, a lot of shit. That's why I don't just answer my door like a normal person anymore. I'm always armed."

As Arryn got closer, she saw blood on parts of the broken

fence, and it furthered her curiosity. "Did someone try to hurt you and your family?"

Elsie pointed toward the men working on the fence. "Those are my sons. I had four sons, and three daughters. Now I have three sons. There are groups of worthless bandits wandering around and taking whatever they want. Two nights ago, they came for the livestock, and my youngest son, Garrett, paid the price."

Arryn's brows furrowed as she looked to the woman with sympathy. Elsie's eyes were locked on her sons repairing the fence. "I'm sorry to hear that. We've heard about bandits lurking around, even fought some, but we thought they were limited to the southern part of the Valley because they seemed to mostly be after the rearick. They'd been attacking their parties and stealing the amphorald crystals used for creating magitech."

"Well, that ain't all they're takin'. They're stealing livestock to feed themselves and tearing up farmland all over. They take whatever they want. The ground here ain't been good for a while now, so I haven't been able to grow a damn thing. The cattle are all we have for income. Milk and meat. And now, two of them are gone, and I have another two knocking on death's door."

"Where are they?" Cathillian asked. "If you take us to them, we can heal them for you. It won't make up for the ones that you lost, but at least you won't lose them, too."

The woman sighed, nodding. "Thank you. I know you came here looking for water for your oversized critters, so it seemed rude to ask. But I do appreciate that."

Elsie yelled for one of her sons, Robbie. As he ran up, his eyes widened just as his mother's had. She waved a hand as he approached. "They're druids, dear. That's her familiar, Snow. She's tame."

The man got a large smile on his face. "Can I pet her?"

Arryn laughed. "Be careful. She might not bite, but she snuggles pretty hard. She's like one of those needy cats that thump your hand when you try to pull it away. Only her paw is like getting smacked with a tree trunk."

In a movement that she was more accustomed to from Zobig than Snow, the big cat growled before pushing against her, nearly knocking her over.

Exasperated, Elsie said, "Robbie, you can pet her all you like while taking her and the Shire down to the pond. Let them get a drink. I'm gonna take these two to the barn."

Realization crossed his face. "Are you guys going to heal the cows?"

Arryn and Cathillian both nodded. "I'm going to look at your land, too," Cathillian said. "I'm betting something in the soil is off, and that's why you can't grow anything. Arryn and I might be able to fix that for you."

As Elsie led Arryn and Cathillian to the barn, the old woman couldn't stop apologizing for bringing them into her family's mess, and thanking the druids for their kindness.

Arryn could tell the old woman was feisty, but losing her son had made her desperate for stability. Experiencing a loss was enough to knock anyone off their path, and having their very livelihood threatened only added insult to injury.

If Arryn and Cathillian could right some of the wrongs that had been done there, they would. But Arryn wanted to go further.

"Do you have any idea where these bastards are staying?" Arryn asked as she laid her hands on the side of a black and white cow with a large gash in her abdomen. How she had survived for two days, Arryn had no idea.

Elsie shook her head. "I heard rumors they were staying farther north, in a large cabin on a lake, but I don't know if that's true. My farm isn't the only one that's been hit. All of us around here have small plots of land; not enough to do much with. We've had to turn to one another for survival."

Arryn smiled. "Well, that ends today. We're heading north

once we leave here. If we come across them—and by '*if*,' I mean '*when*'—you won't have to worry about that anymore. We'll find that cabin and put an end to this."

Elsie's eyes widened as they began to glisten with tears. "You have no idea what that would mean to me, to all of us. Losing my baby, though he was nearly thirty, was the hardest thing I've ever had to do. Losing my husband wasn't even that hard. Those men took our cattle, killed my son, and took our coin. We had quite a lot saved up, and they took every bit of it. If you find a brown leather sack with our brand on it, the same brand on that cow's rear end, you can have it. All of it."

Arryn shook her head. "We're not doing this to get paid. We're doing this because you're good people, and you've lost a lot. You deserve to have someone fighting on your side instead of against you."

Arryn pulled her hands away from the cow, and the animal groaned as she rolled onto her feet, standing up for the first time in two days. The large cow shook her entire body from head to rear, and Arryn could tell she already felt better. Not wanting to waste too much magic, Arryn healed the life-threatening wounds and the infection, but the healing wasn't complete, and further time would be needed. She would still be sore for a couple of days, but she wouldn't be in real pain.

"Young lady, I mean no offense, but those men took that money. It was gone anyway. I would give you that entire sack of coin—and more, if I had it—for what you and your friend did here today. If you go and take care of those men, you deserve every last one of those coins. Like I said, it was gone anyway. Might as well go to whatever it is you're trying to accomplish on your journey. You're obviously far from home."

Arryn nodded. "We're headed north to find a blacksmith that I met there. We need new weapons in the forest because there's a war coming. Dark druids are threatening to take our land and kill our people. That's why we want to help you—because we understand."

Elsie smiled. "And just how do you expect to pay a blacksmith for enough steel to arm the druids of the Dark Forest?"

Giving an awkward laugh, Arryn twisted her hair and tossed it behind her shoulder. "Well, that part was a work in progress."

Elsie stepped forward and took Arryn's hands in hers. "You are a blessing. Take the coins. Buy your steel. If you feel that guilty about it, bring whatever is left back to me. But please make sure your people are taken care of first. You have already taken care of mine; let me do the same for you."

Arryn was overwhelmed by the woman's kindness, and she could see how much it meant to her. Finally, Arryn nodded. "Let's go take a look at that soil of yours. Maybe before we leave here today, we'll actually be able to grow something. I'm betting we can get some vegetables and fruit trees started for you, if you have the seeds. You might even be able to harvest something."

Elsie's eyes widened again. "Really? I prayed for an answer to our hardships, and here you are. Thank you. It's time to start storing up for winter again, and we haven't even been able to grow anything. That would get us through the hard times we'd have coming."

Cathillian nodded as he took a step forward. "Absolutely. I'll take on that task. Arryn needs to conserve the rest of her magic for the journey, but I'll get you going. And then—we're heading north for a hunting trip."

CHAPTER SIX

Arryn and Cathillian traveled well into the night, stopping at a couple of other farms on the way in the hopes of finding out more information on the men they planned to hunt down. The farms were sparse, but they were able to locate them easily enough.

Everyone they asked repeated the very rumors Elsie had heard almost verbatim. They believed them to be in a large cabin on a lake farther north.

That sounded very familiar to Arryn, and she wondered if it might have been one of the many places Talia had stopped with her in tow on the way to dumping her in the Frozen North.

The trip with Talia had been made in several jumps using teleportation. There was no way she could have used so much magic without rest, meaning she had been forced to stop several times. One of those stops was made at what appeared to be a cabin, and Arryn had smelled water close by.

Deep down, she sincerely hoped this cabin was one of those stops. She wanted nothing more than to exact vengeance on them for what they had done to her.

Those monsters had allowed the group of teachers and students to slit her wrists repeatedly to drain her, allowed her assailants to rest and regain strength before allowing them to continue heading north. In truth, Talia was weak enough when stopping at any one of those points, that whoever was there would have been strong enough to overtake her. It pissed Arryn off that no one had tried.

So, she hoped there might be a tiny bit of revenge in this for her, as well as for the old woman, Elsie.

As they approached another cabin, she could see by the moonlight that this one was much larger. A scent filtered through Arryn's nose, and she knew without a doubt that she had been there before. The lake hadn't been well taken care of, and it had a familiar, mossy smell to it along the edges. Also, it was full of fish, but no one ever fished from it, so it emitted a very pungent scent.

"I've been here before," Arryn said. "I'm certain of it. Talia brought me here, which means we are more than likely about to meet physical magic users inside."

Sighing, Cathillian asked, "How do you want to approach this?"

Arryn climbed off Snow's back and took a few steps forward. She placed her hands on the wooden fence. Farther into the field, she could see two black and white cows.

"I bet if we walk over there right now, those cows will be branded with Elsie's mark," Arryn said as she pointed toward the two large, beautiful animals.

Cathillian nodded. "I'd have to say you're probably right about that. So, I refer to my earlier question. How do you want to approach this?"

Arryn's dark eyes flashed green as she reached toward the two cows with her magic. Within an instant, both of them turned and walked toward her. They moved slowly enough not to gather attention, but certainly moved with purpose. As they closed in, she inspected them.

"There it is. The brand." She shook her head as she gave an exasperated huff.

Blackness began to bleed into the whites of her eyes, though her irises were still green. She laid her hands on the top board of the fence, and they grew hot, burning through the wood. Cathillian reached out and caught the board just before it snapped off and thumped loudly into the one just below it. He then threw it off to the side. Leaning down, Arryn repeated the process, and this time, they let the board fall into the tall grass.

"Elsie is waiting for you," she softly told the cows, using her strong affinity for communicating with animals to soothe them. "Head south and go back home." She silently gave them directions, telling them where to go in order to avoid other farms just in case.

Within moments, the cows were on their way, heading out of the pasture to go back home where they belonged.

"Now, time to have some fun," she said.

She and Cathillian quickly made their way toward the cabin, making sure to stay out of view of any windows. The moon was high, and so was the chance they would get caught.

Arryn looked at Cathillian. "I'm going to run inside and cause a scene. You wait out here."

He looked at her incredulously. "I'll do no such thing. I'm going in with you."

She sighed and rolled her eyes, pinching the bridge of her nose. "Now is not the time. I'm a big girl. I know what I'm doing. I have a plan. Just stay out here and wait for my signal, okay?"

"What's the signal?"

She gave a mischievous smile. "Oh, you'll know."

Snow came over and laid down on the ground next to Cathillian. Arryn sent her a silent message to wait outside with him.

Taking a deep breath, Arryn walked around the front of the house, staying under the windows. As she stepped up directly in front of the door, she stood at full height, lifted her right foot, and kicked the door in.

No less than ten people rounded on her with wide eyes. Arryn smiled and waved as she walked in.

Looking around, she saw dinner on the table. Her eyes widened, and she licked her lips and rubbed her belly in an exaggerated manner. "Ah, damn! Dinner? I got here at just the right time! What are you guys having? Steak? What a coincidence... I just let about two tons of steak out of your front yard there," she said, jabbing a thumb toward the now-empty pasture.

Confusion rose on their faces, but was quickly replaced with rage, and they took a few steps forward. A particularly tall one with broad shoulders and red hair stepped out even farther. "What the hell did you just say?"

There was a chair next to the door, and she slid it across the room to the back wall. She made her way over and sat down as each of the men and women stood, looking between themselves and then back over to her.

She crossed her legs, smiling as she clasped her hands in her lap. "Oh, just those two lovely milk cows out there. I recognized the brand and figured they must've gotten lost. It was *so* kind of you to look after them for dear, old Elsie. So, I just went ahead and let them out for you. I figured as poor as all of the other farms in the area seem to be, you didn't need the extra mouths to feed."

The large, red-haired man fumed as he took a few quick steps forward, reaching for a knife in his belt.

Arryn laughed as she raised a finger in the air, moving it back and forth. "Ah, ah, ah!" she said. "I wouldn't do that if I were you, big boy. I promise that you *won't* like the outcome."

"Fuck you, bitch," he said, his eyes flashing black as he brandished his knife.

She sighed and shook her head, the smile never leaving her face. "Well, I *did* warn you."

All ten of them came for her, over half of them flashing black eyes in her direction. Taking a deep breath, she stood, her eyes turning green and black. She threw her hands out in front of her, and magic exploded from them. The wall completely disappeared, the men and women flying through it.

As they all landed hard on the ground, tumbling over backward several times until they flattened, while splinters of wood rained down around them, Cathillian stepped around the corner, leaning against what was left of the wall and crossing his arms.

"I'm assuming that was the signal."

Arryn nodded once as she stepped over the short barrier that remained of the lower part of the wall. She stood on the porch, which was now littered with destroyed wood. "You would assume correctly."

Stepping off the porch, she made her way over to one of the men, who was slowly climbing to his feet. "So, I hear you like stealing things from little old ladies. Is that true?"

He spat at her feet as he wobbled a bit, trying to gain his footing. "Fuck you."

She put her hand over her chest and smiled. "Such poets! Quick, recite me another one." She flung her hand forward, a block of wood flying off the ground and smashing him in the face. "Sorry, sweetheart. You weren't fast enough."

The man crashed to the ground; unconscious or dead, she wasn't certain. One of the women stirred, throwing back some of the debris as she tried to sit up.

"What about you, sweet cheeks?" Arryn asked.

The woman nodded. "We took them. Please, don't kill us."

Cathillian laughed. "You honestly think you have the right to ask that when you took the life of that woman's son? And for what? Livestock?"

"I'm sorry! I didn't mean to! He wouldn't stop coming at us, and I warned him to stop. The others told me to kill him, but I didn't want to!" she said, pleading.

"You lying bitch," another woman said, rolling over onto her stomach as she forced herself up on all fours. "*You're* the one that said that we should kill them all."

"What the hell is going on around here?" Arryn asked. "Are you part of the same group that's been terrorizing the rearick down south? And I would speak right now if I were you, because I don't have much patience."

"*Oooh*," Cathillian said, feigning a chill. "I love it when she gets all sassy like this. I wouldn't test her; I watched her literally rip a woman into six different pieces in the middle of the Arcadian town square, while the whole city watched."

The group seemed visibly shaken. One of them spoke. "Yes. We typically stay up north, but we are part of that group."

"What are you after?" Arryn asked.

The woman who tried to fake her innocence sighed. "The crystals. South of the Heights, there is a group of mercenaries that are collecting all they can. They build their own weapons. They have their own engineers—a few of them, from what I've heard. They take whatever they can, and hire other people to do the rest."

Arryn growled. "How many people has your group killed?"

The woman who had lied before began to tremble when she saw the look on Arryn's face and heard the tone in her voice. She began to shake her head as she tried to back away. "Her son was the only one! I swear it!"

Arryn's eyes flashed black as she lifted her hands up to shoulder-height, and pulled down slightly as she separated ice out from the humidity around her. The crystals formed into long, jagged pieces, which slowly rotated until they were pointing directly at all the people on the ground before her.

A few more of them began to come around then, their eyes widening as they took in the sight before them.

"I'll ask one last time. How many people other than that woman's son have you killed?" she asked again, her voice just as cold as the ice under her control.

"We don't know!" one of the other men said. "Please. Please don't hurt us. It won't happen again, I swear it."

"Was it more or less than ten?" Cathillian asked stepping forward.

When no one answered, Arryn's face turned angry. "More or less?" she barked.

"More!" one of the women shouted, tears streaming down her face. "Way more. We don't know how many because we lost track. But we were hired. It wasn't all of us; the men you want are down south, below the Heights."

Arryn laughed. "*You* were the ones that ended their lives. *You* were the ones that terrorized the hard-working people in this Valley. *You* were the ones that did the dirty work. Therefore, you're *exactly* the ones I'm looking for."

Without saying another word, she jerked her hand forward, sending every jagged piece of ice whistling through the air to impale the bandits, ending them at the same time.

"My, that was dramatic," Cathillian said.

Arryn shook her head. "I'm sick of people taking advantage of those they think are weaker than them. The truth is that those farm families are far stronger than these guys ever could've been. People deserve to live in peace, to raise their families without worrying someone is going to take them away in the blink of an eye."

Cathillian nodded. "I couldn't agree more. That's why I was so happy when you said you would help Elsie. We don't really have the time for it, but the fact that you made time for it truly shows who you are."

Arryn smiled briefly and reached out to give his hand a squeeze. "Now, let's go inside and see if we can't find Elsie's money. I want to give back as much of it as I possibly can, but I know better than to return all of it to her."

Cathillian snorted. "No shit. I'm a little more terrified of her than I am of you, so let's not anger the beast, shall we?"

CHAPTER SEVEN

A blade whistled through the air, stabbing hard into what would be the heart of the target. The loud thump echoed under the canopy, and Celine smiled as she lowered her arm. Leaning back to stand straight again, she looked down at Corrine, who had a large smile on her face.

"It takes some practice, but you can do it. It's easy. Whenever you throw that knife, just imagine the target is the person you hate most in this world. When you do that, the difficulty of it seems to melt away," Celine said.

Elysia pulled a knife from the belt on her hip. Smiling, she stepped forward.

Celine smiled as well. "And after a while, when you really, *really* get into it, then you get to be as good as this woman right here. Watch this."

Celine and Corrine both stepped out of the way, and Elysia turned her back to the target. She had a sly smile on her face as she tossed the knife into the air, letting it flip over before catching it by the point of the blade.

Like lightning, she spun on her heel and threw; the blade cartwheeled through the air and landed with a hard *thump* directly between what would have been the eyes of her target.

Corrine screamed with joy, jumping up and down and clapping her hands. "I want to be that good!" she said, pointing. "Teach me, teach me, teach me."

Celine and Elysia laughed at the girl's excitement. Celine loved watching her. She was getting stronger and stronger all the time. Watching Corrine, she imagined that being around her was similar to what being around Arryn would have been like at that age. She had only been a year older when she arrived in the Dark Forest.

"Arryn is a master with a bow," she informed Corrine. "Other than Elysia, there is no one better in this entire village. I was told that after coming here, but I didn't believe it until I saw it. Arryn's good with a sword, but she's best with projectiles. Today, we're gonna see if you have the same affinity that she does. Are you ready?" Celine asked.

The excitement still had yet to fall from the girl's face as she nodded. A few loose black curls hung around her face; the rest of it was tied back in a thick ponytail. They all bounced when she confirmed her interest.

After retrieving the blade, Celine held it in her hand carefully, the tip of the knife pinched between her thumb and forefinger. She thought back to Samuel, the night he taught her how to throw properly, and how much it had helped her. She called on that wise advice now as she prepared to teach Corrine.

Like Elysia had done, Celine tossed the knife lightly into the air, the blade tumbling over once before she caught it between her thumb and forefinger.

"When you hold the knife, do it with these two fingers." Celine lifted her hand to show her the proper position between her thumb and index finger. She then moved her hand, so the dagger was vertical. "If you hold too tight, it won't spin in the air, which means the blade won't hit the target. If you hold it too loosely, your throw won't have enough force to actually drive it in."

Corrine nodded her head with a deadly serious look on her face as she stared intently on the knife. She focused on it as if it were a coiled snake, ready to strike.

Celine let the hilt of her knife move forward and back toward her wrist. "You should hold tight enough that the blade only barely moves, like this." She tilted her hand back, and the hilt of the knife fell against her wrist. She lifted her arm up over her shoulder. "Don't put your arm too far out, or you'll throw crooked; lift almost directly over your shoulder and throw."

Celine did just that, sending the blade spinning through the air to stick directly into the target, once again hitting it in the chest. Corrine seemed overly excited about Celine hitting her mark.

Elysia handed Corrine a sheath holding six throwing knives. They were small and lightweight—perfect for an eight-year-old girl. "Let's see what you got."

Corrine took the first one out and looked at it, studying it. She put the blade between her two fingers as Celine had showed her, twisting her hand back and forth, getting a feel for the weight and testing it in her hand. She did this repeatedly until she got the pressure right: not too tight, but not too loose.

"Like this?" she asked.

Giving her a reassuring smile, Celine nodded. "Perfect."

Corrine put her left foot forward, raising her right hand above her shoulders. Her elbow was tucked in almost directly in front of her, and Elysia was there to correct, gently moving the girl's elbow out just a bit.

"While your hand should be over your shoulder, your elbow shouldn't be directly in line with it. Otherwise your throw will be uncomfortable, and less powerful. At the same time, you don't want your elbow all the way out to your side, either; doing that will cause your throw to be crooked. Try this position; this should help."

Corrine nodded as Elysia stepped out of the way. The girl took aim at her target and threw… the knife spun through the air several times, until the hilt hit the post just under the target.

Corrine's smile faded as she looked from the post, up to Celine, and then over to Elysia. "I didn't make it."

Elysia smiled. "You just didn't throw hard enough. You also might have held it too loosely. If you hold it just right, it'll flip over once or twice, but it won't have time to do any more. Yours had enough time to turn over again, which allowed the hilt to strike. Try again. This time tighten your grip and throw harder."

Celine's hand was between the girl's shoulder blades, giving her a gentle rub. "And aim just little higher. You're a little shorter because of your age."

Taking a deep breath, Corrine grabbed another throwing knife and took her position, repeating the movements Elysia had just taught her with her elbow. She exhaled before taking another deep breath.

Corrine threw the blade as hard as she could, and it stuck in the lower left corner of the target; not high enough, but it hit hard, even splintering away a piece of the wood.

"Nice!" Celine shouted before grabbing Corrine and pulling her into a hug.

Corrine smiled as she pulled away, looking up with big, emerald green eyes and a smile that could melt ice. "I did it! It wasn't perfect, but I did it!"

Elysia placed her hand on the girl's shoulder, getting her attention. "Now, I want you to practice for the next two hours. You just hit your target, so I know you can do it. I have to go teach another class, but I want this to be your focus for the day."

"Why won't I be training with the other kids?" she asked, a little confused.

Elysia knelt before her. "You said you want to be able to

protect yourself, and you want a good start on being the best warrior this forest has ever seen, right?"

Corrine nodded passionately. "Yes! I want to be the best."

Elysia nodded. "Here's the honest situation. You want to be able to protect yourself. You want to be able to defend yourself, and anyone else, if danger comes. Unfortunately, you are still too small to be able to adequately defend yourself in hand-to-hand combat. You can put up one hell of a fight, but against a full-grown man, it's not likely to do any good."

Corrine's eyes turned toward the ground as she nodded. "Oh."

"However, you are more than old enough, and more than big enough, to throw a blade with expert precision. You are woman enough to take a man down to the ground if he comes for you, as long as we properly teach you how to handle a knife. Do you understand?" Elysia asked.

Corrine seemed confused. "I... I think?"

Celine knelt next to Elysia, reached out, and took one of Corinne's hands. "What she's saying is that she's giving you what you want. If she puts you in that class exclusively, you'll learn how to protect yourself *in the future*, but it won't do you any good until you're older, because you're not big enough to fight an adult right now. Learning how to use a knife is something that you *can* do, and the one way that you *can* protect yourself and others."

Elysia smiled. "I couldn't have said it better myself. Apparently, I didn't say it better at all." She laughed, and Celine and Corrine followed suit. "I know you're capable of taking care of yourself. That's why I'm making this exception for you. You'll still train with the other students, but I also want you doing this. But let this be known: if you fall behind in your combat training, we will end these extra classes, and you'll train just like the other kids. Is that understood?"

Corrine seemed to be quite a bit more excited now, understanding more of what was happening around her. She nodded her head with a smile. "I understand. I promise I won't let you down."

Elysia smiled, resting her hand on the side of the girl's face. "I know you won't."

BAST AND CLEO had been staying with the druids for several days, and in that time, they had learned quite a lot. They were voracious fighters, just like the men at home. Where they had come from, the soldiers trained day in and day out. The women had only recently joined their ranks, but they were equally as ruthless, once given the chance.

The twins had been investigating the druid's defenses, and had ideas of their own for reinforcing them. After all, three to six-inch-long thorns were terrifying, but if someone was skilled enough, or determined enough, a battle axe or longsword could defeat it.

"I can feel the earth beneath us. There's plenty of stone to build a great wall," Cleo said.

Bast nodded as she stared up to the top of the barrier that separated the druids of the Dark Forest from the rest of the forest. "The dark druids have found their way through this barrier too many times, it seems. Alexander will never keep them out indefinitely if they don't do something else."

"The thing is, if we convince them to do the stone wall, it'll do exactly what they want it to: it will keep out any nature magic users. And if it's erected on the other side of this wall of thorns, this one will still keep out any physical magic users who managed to break through the stone. If we make it several feet thick, a mix of stone and compacted earth, their barrier will be nearly thirty feet thick. No one would be able to pass through without their knowledge."

Bast exhaled, shaking her head. "Thirty feet. That seems

excessive, but if this war doesn't end, they'll need it. But it would block them inside. We would have to teach them physical magic."

"Not a chance," Ryel said as he approached from behind.

Cleo turned. "Are you saying you would turn down a stronger barrier simply because you don't want to learn physical magic?"

He smiled. "You didn't even know the type of magic you use was classified as physical until you came here. You haven't seen the destruction of physical magic; the Chieftain will never agree to it."

Bast looked toward the wall. "Seems that times are changing around here. From what I heard, outsiders haven't been allowed in for decades, yet here we are. The army from the city north of Arcadia was sheltered here. Arcadians are still here. Even a dark druid child is here. The Chieftain is becoming more diverse as the opportunity for peace continues to blossom. I think you might be surprised what he'd agree to."

Nodding, Ryel said, "We are masters of our magic. It's just who we are. We aren't opposed to having stronger walls, but the physical magic bit would all fall on Arryn. Perhaps we could just talk with the Chieftain, but I think that you'd be much better off talking to Arryn and having her approach him."

Bast smiled and shrugged. "If you say so." She looked around. "I would be honored to build it with her. From what we hear, she's quickly becoming a master of both branches."

CHAPTER EIGHT

Amelia flipped a chair around backward, straddling it as she sat across the jail cell. The prisoner was still healing from the battle she and Bast had taken part in with the rearick brothers, Ren and Sven. The young woman had paralyzed the man during the fight with one of her powerful punches.

After bringing him back to Arcadia, Amelia was able to find someone that had learned enough from Arryn and Cathillian to heal the prisoner of his affliction, but they had only healed the bones. The nerve damage was only partially resolved, as the magic user wasn't nearly as skilled in nature magic as they were in combat.

The man was able to walk and take care of himself, but not without the aid of crutches. His legs were too weak to stand without them.

Amelia smiled, though it was meant to be more threatening than anything. "So, tell me a bit about yourself. Where are you from? What's your favorite color? Why the fuck are you stealing from my city and the people I employ? You know, the basics."

The man gave a sarcastic laugh, shaking his head. "I ain't telling you shit. You're cute, but you ain't *that* cute."

Sighing, Amelia said, "Look... This is going to go one of two ways. Either you're going to give me the information that I want peacefully, or I'm going to bring someone in here who is far worse than you, and I'm going to let them have fun."

His eyes widened a bit, but then he laughed. "I highly doubt that. You're not the type."

A wicked smile spread across her lips. "You're right, I'm not." Her eyes flashed black as she slowly lifted her hand in a graceful motion, her elbow coming to rest on the back of the chair. She snapped a finger, and the cuffs of his pants lit on fire. "Well, I'm not the type to let someone else do my dirty work, anyway."

The man screamed as he reached down, struggling fruitlessly to put out the flames.

With a wave of Amelia's hand, the fire went away, and she relaxed into position again. "Now, shall we play nicely? Because I have a city to protect, and I'm not going to let scum like you threaten us. We have been through too much, and my ability to give a damn is broken. I'll play the bad guy if it means protecting the people who depend on me."

"You're fucking crazy, lady!" he shouted, inspecting his ankle. It was red, but there weren't any blisters. Amelia had been careful to keep the fire from burning too hot, and his freakout had kept it from burning into his leg.

Rolling her eyes, she said, "Oh, please do keep telling me all the wonderful things about myself. It doesn't make me want to set you on fire again at all."

She gave him a stern look, and he swallowed hard, sitting back and nodding.

"I'm going to ask you one more time." She sighed as she stared into his cold eyes. "What is going on in the Valley?"

Rolling his eyes, he threw his hands in the air before letting them fall back into his lap. "Well, seeing as how I'm never getting out of here, and none of those bandits are going to risk coming into the city to get to me, I suppose I'm safe enough. The guy's name you want is Locke. He's an asshole, and I quite despise him, but he pays well."

"Who is Locke, and what does he have to do with this?" she asked.

"Locke used to be an Arcadian guard. When Adrien fell, a lot of people left the city; that included a lot of the Arcadian guards. They fled south, hoping like hell not to run into Hannah. They kept going until they were on the south side of the Heights. They have an encampment there. They started out doing dirty work for the nobles, taking care of nuisances, acting as hired guns for government assholes who wanted towns kept in line. Now they're in business for themselves."

She really didn't like the sound of that.

"Is Arcadia at risk of them attacking?"

He laughed. "Did you hear a thing I just said? They don't want anything to do with Arcadia. That's why everybody working for Locke stays far away from the city. We try to stay off your radar as much as possible. Obviously, that didn't go as planned."

"Yes, well, that's pretty hard to do when you are attacking caravans every day, and taking the product I've been ordering."

He shrugged. "I suppose you're right, but still... The city has nothing to worry about from Locke. Just the rearick."

"So, when you say Locke is in business for himself, what do you mean?"

"They have their own engineers, and they're stealing the crystals to make magitech weapons. They're stockpiling them. They sell them to other assholes who want to take advantage of the little guy, to those same government assholes that used to hire them, or they just use them to take what they want. Last I heard, Locke wanted to start building his own city."

Amelia shook her head. "No doubt built off the backs of those who can't help themselves."

The man smiled. "Naturally."

Hearing all of this made her angry. It made her angry because she wanted to do something about it, but she couldn't. She couldn't leave the city, and she couldn't send guards, either. If facing a large group of well-trained soldiers, her guards would never stand a chance.

The Arcadian Guard was feared in the Valley—even outside of it, when Adrien had been around. They were ruthless, extremely skilled fighters, and everyone knew not to mess with them.

With the Cella governor's help, that was slowly becoming the case again. He was taking her undertrained guards and putting them through rigorous combat training until they were capable of practicing on their own to better their skills. The first group that had returned to her was infinitely stronger than when they had left.

Their feared name would once again be theirs to have, only they wouldn't be ruthless. Not unless their enemy truly was an enemy.

There had to be a way to stop them, but she didn't know how. The only thing that she could think of was the twins. They had crossed that very water the bandits' encampment rested on now. She wondered just how close they had gotten, and exactly how that would have gone if the bandits had attacked them.

She almost laughed at the thought. Those girls were powerful, and she knew from personal experience that Bast literally could've ripped them apart.

She decided that sending a letter might be best. She still had Ash, and she was getting better and better at communicating with him. He was a very smart boy, and she knew she might be able to get the raven to fly a letter to the Dark Forest.

Maybe after everything was all said and done, and the war in the Dark Forest was over, Arryn would be willing to fight on behalf of Arcadia again.

ALARIC AND JERICK had been traveling with their people for days. They could no longer stay in the southern part of the Dark Forest, and traveling farther into the Arcadian Valley was impossible. The only option they had was to head west, toward the Terresian plains.

Even returning to the Terres Forest was out of the question while Alexander was still alive. Alexander would be anticipating that move, and they would be dissolved entirely.

The only option was to move west in hopes of finding people they could recruit. They would need all the help they could get.

As the moon rose high over the fields, they had finished making camp for the night. Alaric decided to keep the first watch, only a three-hour shift, and Jerick would take the next.

Off in the distance, he could hear cattle calling out to one another as they grazed. There were several lying on the ground not far from them, but far enough that the animals felt comfortable. Alaric was well aware of any creature's discontent at their presence.

Unlike the druids of the Dark Forest, animals were not innately attracted to them; they feared the dark druids, and wanted to stay far away.

Alaric's pointed ears twitched as the sound of a broken stick echoed. His whitish grey-green eyes narrowed as he looked around, his senses picking up the presence of several people approaching.

Keeping low, Alaric went to his brother's tent and kicked his foot. Without saying a word, Jerick sat up, his eyes focusing on his brother.

"We have company," Alaric warned, his voice low.

Jerick quickly got out of the tent, following his brother just outside of the camp. They saw something glowing approaching—several somethings. As that something drew closer, the brothers quickly realized there were a dozen or so men carrying magitech weapons.

"How exactly do we get out of this one?" Jerick asked.

Alaric smiled. "By proving *we're* the biggest threat."

Without hesitation, Alaric began to walk toward their targets. He felt for their energy and realized the weapons were their only talent; they had no magical control. At least, they didn't seem to. It was possible they thought they were walking up on travelers who had no access to magic.

It was no matter, though. He had no worries.

"Cooperate, and you'll be just fine," came a voice from the path ahead of him. "Piss me off, and I'll make sure you regret it."

Alaric laughed, his brother doing the same. "We'll see about that."

Jerick's arm lifted. Vines burst through the ground and wrapped around their weapons. He flung his hand aside, sending each of the weapons flying several feet away to land on the ground.

Alaric stepped forward, his eyes flashing as his hand extended outward. Each of the men immediately began to start feeling fatigued, and pain radiated through their bodies as Alaric used his death touch. He knew he wouldn't be able to use it for long, as it would drain him entirely, but he had enough in him to make them feel like they were dying. It would be enough to establish him as the dominant figure.

"I think it's *you* who shouldn't piss *me* off," Alaric said, his voice cold.

He released his hold on them, and they fell to the ground. He was thankful for the darkness, as it hid the fatigue he knew would be showing on his face. Each of them breathed heavily as they doubled over on the ground, unable to do anything except be grateful they were still alive.

"Introductions are usually customary upon meeting," Alaric said. "I'm Alaric, and this is my brother Jerick. We would like to know who the hell you are, and why you thought trying to overpower us was a good idea. Clearly, that didn't work out for you."

With a flick of his wrists, Jerick bound each of their hands and feet. Even when they recovered, they would be unable to run. "I would answer him if I were you."

"We wanted to see if you had any magitech on you," one of them said breathlessly. "We came from south of the Heights. We never run into people while coming through, and thought this was a lucky break."

Alaric laughed. "For me, this *is* very lucky."

The men all looked at him with obvious confusion. The moonlight casting directly down on the field illuminated their faces.

"You see, I am fighting a war that I'm having a hard time winning. I've been fighting the same battle for decades. I think it's time that things are turned in my favor. How would you like to join me? You seem rather stupid, but that can be fixed with training—proper training, that is."

The men struggled against their bonds, and the same one spoke again. "We can't join you. We already work for someone, and he would destroy us for betraying him."

Alaric's eyes narrowed as a dark smile grew. If there was another in control of them, that might mean there were even more men he could recruit. *The more, the merrier.* He would only need to be taken to them to establish himself as the dominant figure.

He looked to the magitech weapons and then back to them. "You said you were coming for us, hoping we had magitech weapons? Does he have you do this often?"

"Trust me, buddy. You don't want to go messing with Locke. He's not someone to fuck with. He has an arsenal of magitech weapons, every kind you could possibly think of, and more are being built over time. If you go in there, he'll kill you. And I don't mean that lightly. I mean you will be captured and then killed as slowly as humanly possible. It's the same thing he'll do to us if we betray him."

Alaric shrugged. "What if you didn't betray him? What if you simply took us to have a meeting with him? Surely, that couldn't be out of the question, right?"

The leader looked to his men before cautiously looking back to Alaric. "What exactly do you have in mind?"

Sighing, Jerick said. "It boils down to preservation, boys. You can take us to Locke, and risk dying by his hand—though a meeting isn't all that terrible, so you probably wouldn't—or you can be guaranteed death here. And I promise, Alaric's death touch is quite painful, and I use other methods in which a painful death is certain, but excruciatingly slow. Your friend Locke and I have that in common. Do we understand each other?"

The man sighed, grinding his teeth as he shook his head. "Fine. We'll take you, but I can't promise you'll come back."

CHAPTER NINE

Christopher tossed and turned, sweat beading on his forehead as he felt the rocks digging into his side and back, pain radiating through his entire body. His stomach felt like someone had reached inside, grabbed a handful of his intestines, and had begun to squeeze and twist.

This was a new poison. It was different than the rest; it caused intense pain, while he was forced to endure it with a fully conscious mind. He wanted to throw up. He wanted to heave every drop of it from himself, but he couldn't. The poison took so long to work that it was long gone out of his stomach, and was already coursing through his body.

"How does that feel?" Aeris asked. "Does it feel painful? Is it agonizing? It certainly looks that way, but I want to hear you say it. I want to hear you scream."

Christopher didn't want to give him what he wanted. He didn't want to scream or cry out. He wanted to die. He prayed to whoever might be listening that they end his life, end his suffering. He prayed for Arryn's safety, but after enduring this pain for so many years, he couldn't do it anymore. He couldn't stay alive for even one more day. He could feel himself giving up.

Aeris, angry that Christopher wouldn't give in, lashed out. He kicked him hard in the back, earning the scream that he had so desired from his victim. "There it is," Aeris said, a dark joyfulness in his voice.

"Please! Please stop!" Christopher cried out as he jerked away from another kick. In doing so, Aeris' boot grazed his side, tearing open the skin and exposing him even more.

"Christopher." He heard an angelic voice in the darkness, but couldn't find it. He searched, his tear-filled eyes frantically looking around for it.

"Listen to my voice, Christopher. You're safe. This is a dream. Turn now and face him. Face your captor."

He still felt terrified; his entire body shook as he heaved breaths, tears streamed down his face. He could feel the blood running down his back, and he couldn't understand how it could possibly be a dream.

"This is a nightmare of your own creation," the voice soothed. "You allow your subconscious to control you, but *you* are in control. Turn now and take that control back from him."

Slowly, Christopher turned, his eyes coming to rest on Aeris' angry face. The dark druid jumped forward, kicking him again hard in the side. Christopher cried out as he gripped the spot that Aeris' boot had torn open just a moment before.

"I can't! I can't. It's real..." He sobbed again, shaking his head. How many times had he convinced himself he was dreaming? How many times had he convinced himself he was crazy? This time was no different.

"You aren't going anywhere," Aeris said. "You're here with me forever."

The room seemed to lighten a bit as the angelic voice once again swept through the cave. "He is just a man, as are you. But the man you face here—the man that torments you still—is *dead*. He can *never* hurt you again. Arryn saw to that, remember?"

Arryn...

He remembered his beautiful daughter. She was so sunshiny and sweet, running around in her little dresses, and playing with her dolls. Such a beautiful child—and so smart, too. Just like her mother.

But then he remembered someone else. A woman, fully grown, long, beautiful black hair reaching all the way down her back, and a strong, well-built body, achieved by years of rigorous combat training. He saw her eyes: a terrifying glimpse of black and green as the wind began to swirl and the skies began to darken.

Arryn. My little girl.

Slowly, things began to come back to him. He looked up from the ground, quickly finding the eyes of his captor. "You're dead."

Aeris laughed. "Excuse me? How can I be dead when I'm right here with you?" he once again jumped forward, kicking out at Christopher's face.

Only this time, Christopher caught his foot.

Aeris' eyes widened as he watched the man rise to his knees, still holding his foot. Christopher pulled, and Aeris went flying forward. Christopher caught him by the throat and slammed him down to the ground before straddling him.

"Years! You took *years* from me! I could've found her long ago, if you would have just let me go. I could have been with her. I could've given her the father she needed while growing up! You took *everything* from me." He paused and then a dark smile crossed his face. "But she repaid the favor. She gave you exactly what you deserved."

The room seemed to grow warmer then, the heat washing through him as he felt his hands gripping at nothing. Aeris had disappeared, and the world around him was dramatically changing.

He was standing in an open field, watching his daughter call upon her power. It had been unlike anything he had ever seen. Not even his beautiful late wife had been able to use so much.

"She's stronger than I ever could've imagined," he said to himself.

"And you gave that to her," came the angelic voice again. He looked to his right to see Zoe standing next to him. It had been her voice speaking to him the whole time, guiding him. "Your sacrifice gave her the power to save thousands. If you hadn't done what you did, thousands would have remained enslaved. It was because of you that she grew up the way she did. Let go of the demons that tell you otherwise. You did not fail her; you gave her every tool she needed to succeed."

He gasped as his eyes flew open, and he sat bolt upright in bed. Elysia was sitting at the foot, her eyes glowing, and her hands on his ankles, pushing warmth through him as Zoe sat on the floor next to him, her eyes white as she held his hand.

Each of the women let go, pulling back and allowing her eyes to fade back to their normal color. Zoe gave him a soft smile. "Welcome back. How do you feel?"

Christopher reached up and wiped his forehead. He couldn't believe how well that had worked. He had been suffering from nightmares for years, and waking up in the morning still inside of them.

Now he was freed, and he awoke to kindness and support.

It had been Zoe's idea for Christopher to sleep and allow her to navigate his dreams. She was curious to see if she could heal the parts of his brain still affected by the trauma.

The dream he had experienced was a memory of something that had once happened. Aeris had ordered Jace to poison Christopher, hoping it would drive him permanently insane; but the substance had no mental effects whatsoever. It only physically tortured him.

Zoe had navigated through the dream along with him, while linking Elysia in as well. Once Elysia was able to feel the pain, she began to push her healing power through him. While it wasn't nearly as effective as Zoe coaching him to face the man he feared so much, he certainly felt much better.

Perhaps the effects of both were something to explore more.

"How do you feel?" Zoe asked.

He took a couple of deep breaths, trying to still his racing heart. "Triumphant. Like I defeated him."

Elysia rubbed a gentle hand over his ankle. "That's what we were hoping for. I'll be honest; I don't know anything about the mind or how it works. This is all a first for me, but I'm open to try anything. I would love to see you succeed, Christopher."

He smiled as he looked at her with warmth. "Thank you. More than you know."

"You mean a lot to Arryn, and therefore you mean a lot to me. You're a good man, and you have proven yourself to be a man worth saving. I hope to once again look into the eyes of the man who protected my son and his daughter while his wife fought off a lycanthrope. I know that with a little more work, we will meet again."

Christopher was almost brought tears again as he thought about being that strong. He wanted to take up sword fighting again, but he was afraid to ask. He was afraid to stand with the other warriors of the tribe, knowing he might not have it in him anymore.

He also worried he might have some sort of flashback and freak out. It would take time, but he was willing to do whatever it took to get his mind back and be everything his daughter needed.

Smiling, he said, "I think I'll go to the pit today and watch all the classes."

Elysia smiled. "You'll do better than that. I think today you'll help me on the side. We'll hand out weapons, and call out winners—together."

His smile grew, liking that even more. He nodded. "Sounds like fun."

CHAPTER TEN

After leaving the cabin, Arryn and Cathillian had headed directly north. It took the rest of the night, but they found a small village where Arryn had been kept on her way to the mountain. It was the same village where she had stopped and met the blacksmith upon her return.

When they reached the small, modest house she was looking for, she dismounted. Turning to Snow, she gave her a scratch behind the ear and down her jawline as she liked, before kissing the side of her head.

"Thank you, Snow," Arryn said and made her way to the door.

"You sure this is the one?" Cathillian asked stepping up beside her.

Arryn nodded. "Oh, yeah. Can't forget it."

She reached up, knocking three times before lowering her hand. It was early morning, so she wasn't sure if he would be inside, or in the shop somewhere. She was about to knock again when the door opened.

Shock and then recognition registered on the man's face. "Arryn?" he asked, smiling. "You're back!"

She smiled and nodded. "I am. This time I brought a friend. Roger, this is Cathillian. Cathillian, Roger."

Cathillian placed his fist over his chest, saluting him in a way his own people did, but Roger just extended his hand. Cathillian smiled and took it to shake.

"Nice to meet you. Arryn spoke very highly of you, and I appreciate you helping her when she was on her way back from the mountain," Cathillian said.

The smith pulled his hand back, waving off the comment. "It was no problem at all. She needed help, and after what I knew she'd been through, I figured it was the least I could do. Bitch and Bastard!" He exclaimed as his eyes wandered between the two of them to see Snow.

Arryn laughed, stepping out of the way.

"Is that her? Is that the same tiger you had before? She's huge! She's even bigger than she was when I last saw you!"

"Apparently, that's the magic of being a familiar. You should see her baby. He hadn't gotten any bigger than what you saw, not even an inch, until last week. He's been growing like a weed since then," she said.

Roger laughed, stepping back, out of the way. "You guys are more than welcome to come in. Snow, you can, too, if you can fit through the door."

Snow grumbled at him, but she managed to squeeze through. She walked into the main room and flopped down on the floor, using her claws to rake the rug up under her head to use as a pillow.

Arryn rolled her eyes and shook her head at the sight.

"So, what brings you guys all the way up here? Not that I'm not happy to see you; I'm actually very happy to see you made it through. I assume you were successful, yes?" Roger said.

Arryn nodded. "I was very successful. I killed Talia that very night; the mystic she had working with her, I went back for later."

He smiled. "Good. I'm glad you were able to help your people. After you survived everything that you did, I had no doubt you'd make it."

She looked to Cathillian for a moment before turning back to the blacksmith. "Actually, we came here because we've been met with another challenge."

Roger was in the kitchen area, putting water in a pot to boil over the fire. "Challenge? What are you up to now?"

"We recently suffered an attack from a tribe of dark druids who want to take the Dark Forest for themselves. We lost several people in the attack, including our blacksmith and his apprentice, and all of our weapons are shot from constant training and use."

Roger listened as Arryn told him about the many battles they had already faced, how often their people trained, and that another battle was coming soon.

"Well, I'm glad you came to me, then. I'm sorry it got so bad for you, but we'll get this taken care of now," he assured her with a smile.

As they made their way to the shop behind the house, Arryn looked around, thinking about the last time she had been there. "Whatever happened to the widow?"

The widow was the nickname given to Talia's mother. She'd had many husbands who had all met with mysterious deaths. Everyone believed she had been the cause, but it had been Talia, her daughter. She had begun killing them as young as five. Her obsession with her insane father, Adrien, had driven her to do unbelievable things—even as a child.

Roger smiled and shook his head. "You wouldn't even recognize her. You freed her that day."

Arryn's brows furrowed, planting confusion on her face. "How do you mean? I'm assuming you're talking about Talia's death, but how did she change?"

"After you left, I invited her inside to sit with me. Given that her child was about to be killed, and she had helped in taking her down, I figured she could use a friend. I made her a cup of tea, and she opened up about what it was like to raise her. It seems all the rumors were true.

"We talked for several hours, and then suddenly, it was like night and day. One second we were chatting, and she seemed just as she always had whenever I had run into her. The next, tears welled in her eyes and she began to cry. When I asked her what was wrong, all she said was, 'It's done. It's over.'"

Arryn was taken aback. "She knew when I killed her?"

He shrugged. "I don't understand it, either. I don't know if she has a form of mental magic, or if it was just mother's intuition. Either way, she said she could just feel it."

Arryn nodded. Roger led them into the shop, and he went to work firing up the forge. Arryn looked around, admiring how well everything was set up and how organized it was. "How has she been since then?"

He grabbed a long piece of steel from the barrel and laid it out on the table while waiting for the fire to get hot enough. "She's been great. She goes to the marketplace with the hood of her cloak down. She talks to people and smiles now. It's like she's a brand new person. She said it feels like she'd been asleep this whole time, and now she's finally awake."

Arryn snorted. "I would certainly imagine so. I would assume it to be more like being stuck in a nightmare for thirty years, and someone finally coming along and waking you. I'm glad she's doing well. I thought about her a few times, but I tried not to dwell on it. It was rather depressing, knowing I had to speak to a mother and tell her I was about to execute her daughter. She knew how horrible Talia was, though."

Brushing a few stray hairs off her face, Arryn clapped her hands together and smiled. "Enough about that. What can I do to help? I can create more steel, if you need it."

He nodded. "If you need an order as big as you say, I'm definitely gonna need some help. Why don't you go out back? There is a pile of stones back there. I like those in particular, because they transmogrify quite a bit easier than other things."

Pointing to the long piece of steel laying on the table, he said, "If you can, create pieces of steel like this. If you want smaller weapons, like daggers, use the smaller stones." He looked to Cathillian. "If you want, you can go out back with her. There are several trees back there that I cut branches from for hilts."

Cathillian nodded. "Sure. I can see about growing you a few extra trees, too, if you'd like."

Roger smiled. "That would be great, thank you."

Between Arryn and Cathillian, they were easily able to craft the bare bones for dozens of swords. She was able to create pieces of steel in varied lengths, and Cathillian was easily able to break the wood down into smaller chunks that could be filed into the shape of a handle.

By the end of the night, even after an afternoon nap for all of them, they had created quite a lot of what they needed. But it took another day and well into the evening to finish.

"I'm not gonna lie," Arryn said as she looked over the large pile of weapons that were now lying in the cart. "You're kind of a badass. These blades are even better than the ones we had before, and you did this way faster than our smiths were ever able to."

Cathillian laughed. "Yeah, you want a job? You can come live in the Dark Forest with us for a while."

He and Roger laughed, but Arryn's face was serious as she looked to Roger. "Actually, that's not a bad idea. We don't have a blacksmith now, and I'm betting if you took a few teenage apprentices, they would be able to learn easier than the adults. If they learned the physical magic necessary, they could craft just as quickly, but I don't see that happening. That part would have to fall on me. I've learned a lot today about smithing, but not enough that I would feel comfortable to go back and teach anyone how to do it."

Roger's face turned serious as he thought over her words. "Really? Go to the Dark Forest?"

Arryn nodded. "Absolutely. It might be a while, but once the war is all over, we really need to train new blacksmiths. At the very least, you can teach them how to do the hammering and all that good stuff, and teach me more about transmogrifying. That way, I can help them. The first time I ever successfully did it was on that mountain; this was the second time. You're apparently a great teacher, and I can definitely use the tutoring."

His expression turned thoughtful for a moment, and then he started to nod. "Sure. Why not? I've always wanted to know what it was like in the Dark Forest; especially after meeting you, and now your friend. You're not nearly as scary as I thought you would be."

Cathillian's eyes widened. "What? Not scary? Well, now you're just being rude."

Arryn rolled her eyes at him, and the trio made their way inside. Roger made them a hearty stew and some tea. They sat and ate for quite some time, talking about what they might accomplish in the Dark Forest.

Suddenly Snow perked up, immediately heading for the door.

Everyone seemed alarmed except for Arryn, who had a natural bond with the big cat. She could feel Snow's excitement—not worry or apprehension.

Arryn stood and made her way to the door. A light scratching noise echoed through the room just before she made it there. When she opened the door, she looked down and saw a very familiar white rabbit.

Her face lit up in a big smile. "Sir Fluffenstuffs!" she shouted before leaning down and stretching out her hands.

A fat, white rabbit hopped forward, rushing into her arms.

She picked him up and kissed his head, snuggling him close to her face as she closed the door. Snow came over and gave the rabbit a couple of sniffs before giving him a wet kiss on his soft cheek.

Though Arryn could sense the tiny amount of fear that the rabbit still held for Snow, she could feel his happiness about seeing them, as well.

Roger laughed. "I see you found Rodney," he said.

Arryn scrunched up her face, looking from him down to the rabbit. "Your name is *Rodney*?" Looking back up to Roger, she asked, "What kind of name is *Rodney* for a rabbit?"

He quirked an eyebrow at her. "What kind of animal master leaves her rabbit behind?"

She pointed a finger at him. "Hey! I'm not a master of *all* animals. We only bond to one… Well, I guess I bonded to two, but still. That's not the point. He was just my best friend up there; I didn't want to rip him away from his home and put him in the forest where he didn't belong. I did it for his own good."

"Yeah, well, that rabbit has been here since you left. He wanders back up north sometimes, but for the most part he's here in the village. That's why he's so chubby. Everyone loves him, so they feed him constantly."

She looked down and smiled, rolling him over on his back in her arms against his will so she could scratch his belly. Though he didn't like it, he let her do it anyway. "You came down here and stayed? You poor thing. And on top of that, you were given a name like Rodney. That man clearly has no talent for names."

"What would you have named him?" Roger asked.

Shrugging, Arryn said, "Fluffbutt. Sir Fluffenstuffs, which I *lovingly* used upon seeing him. Twinklenose. Monsieur Hopsalot Von Fuzzypants. There are just *so* many, and you chose fucking *Rodney*." She shook her head and *tsked* at him.

Roger stood there, staring at her incredulously, jaw slightly agape, clearly unable to believe she had just made up all those names at a moment's notice. "There's something severely wrong with you, isn't there?"

Cathillian laughed, clapping Roger on the back. "You know, there isn't a day that goes by that I don't ask myself that very question about her."

Arryn flipped the rabbit back over, sitting him down on the floor so he could visit with Snow. The tiger had flopped down on a rug, and the rabbit cautiously made his way over and snuggled into her thick fur. Snow threw her arm around him, scooping him in closer, making sure she didn't put too much weight on him.

"What's the plan from here?" Roger asked.

Arryn had been staring lovingly at the animals lying on the floor. She turned to Roger, bringing herself back to the present. She took a few steps back into the kitchen, sitting down at the table.

"Well, we're gonna finish eating. I guess we should probably take a nap before we start back, because we really have used a lot of magic." She pulled a bag of coins out of her pocket and placed it on the table. "And if anything is left after you take what you want out of that, I'm going to return it to the little old lady it was stolen from."

Roger held the bag in his hands, looking at her suspiciously. "You stole this? That certainly doesn't sound like a very noble and Arryn-like thing to do. Then again, it's not like I know you *that* well."

Arryn looked at him like he was a crazy person. "Are you serious? Hell no, I didn't steal that. Well, I guess *technically* I did. But the bad guys stole it from a little old lady after killing her son. I promised I would return it, but she demanded we take payment out of it, because if we hadn't come along, the money was gone anyway, and she wanted to thank us for healing their cows, giving them crops, and she wanted to thank us for healing her cows and growing them some crops."

He nodded, opening the bag. "While I do need the extra money, I would feel terrible for taking it. Not only from you, but also from the woman."

Arryn sighed. "I don't think you understand just how serious she was."

Cathillian laughed. "Yeah, she was quite feisty about it. Arryn is likely to get a thump if we return and no money is missing from the bag."

Arryn's jaw dropped as she looked at him. "Why just me? Why not you, too?"

He gave an exaggerated smile. "Because she's scary! I'd run like hell. If my mama ever taught me anything, it was don't mess with a woman with a personality like that. When she says something, you damn well listen."

Arryn's expression changed to one of disbelief. "If that's so, then you should probably be afraid of me, too."

He nodded. "Oh, I'm well aware. I'm just hoping she knocks your ass out, because I'll be running. I'll stand in front of a lycanthrope for you any day, but not a feisty woman. Sorry, you're on your own."

Roger laughed, and Arryn just shook her head.

"I'm glad the two of you came by. It makes me happy to see you're doing so well. I see why you were so anxious to get back home. You have good people in the Dark Forest. I'd be happy to join your people there once your battle has been won. I say 'when' because I have no doubt in my mind you guys will triumph."

"Thank you, Roger," Cathillian said, giving him a traditional druid salute. To Arryn's surprise, Roger returned it.

They sat in silence then, finishing up their stew before settling in to get some sleep. The day had been long, and the magic use a bit heavy. While Arryn didn't anticipate running into any more issues on the way home, she definitely didn't want to take the chance of it happening while she might be too weak to fight.

She, Cathillian, Snow, and Chaos could rest for a little while longer. She wanted to leave after midnight. This time, if the rabbit decided to come with her, she didn't plan to stop him.

But his name wasn't going to be fucking *Rodney*.

CHAPTER ELEVEN

The bandits who had made the mistake of strolling into the dark druid territory had been busy leading the dark druids to the land they called home. The path they had to take was much longer than simply going up and over the mountain, but that was necessary because of the heavy rearick population, as well as the mystics.

They didn't want to take a chance on running into either one of them and word somehow getting back to Arryn or Alexander. Instead, they followed the same path the bandits had taken, around the western side of the mountains and then heading southeast. Once they reached the edge of the sea, they would follow it until they reached their town.

As they neared the encampment, Alaric heard the sounds of hammers striking and saw smoke billowing up ahead.

One of the bandits, noticing the concern on his face, said, "Don't worry about that. That's normal. That's one of the smith shops. We have several."

Alaric smiled, choosing silence as he thought over the possibilities of what might happen there. Up ahead, they saw a tall, wooden gate. It was poorly crafted, and had obviously been put together in a rush. Alaric imagined it was more for letting people know they were not to approach, rather than actually serving as a functional way to keep people out.

If anyone really tried, they could get in with no problem.

"Will you go and tell your master that we've arrived?" Jerick asked.

The bandit laughed. "Are you serious? No offense, but if you think for an instant that having us along with you is going to buy you favor with Locke, you are very mistaken. He'll kill all of us on principle alone."

Jerick shrugged. "I don't really think that's going to be a problem. They will be gravely mistaken if they attack us, I can assure you of that."

Several small thumps sounded out in front of them as a single barrage of arrows landed in their path.

The bandit shook his head, sighing. "Well, I guess, let the games begin."

"What the hell are you doing here?" one of the men on the wall asked. "You brought outsiders with you?"

The bandit shook his head. "I didn't exactly have a choice in the matter. They want to see Locke."

The man standing on the wall laughed. "Locke? You really *have* lost your mind. You know as well as I do he doesn't entertain guests." The man on the wall turned his head to look on either side of him, nodding in each direction. All archers lifted their bows. "Kill them and be done with it. That includes those two dumbasses."

Alaric laughed, his brother following suit. Both stepped forward. Jerick flipped his hand, causing a vine to shoot up through the ground and wrap around the man's neck. The other men standing on the wall were in shock, staring with wide eyes.

Jerick swung his hand from left to right, the vine throwing his victim first to the left, then to the right, creating a domino effect and knocking them to the floor of the wall.

He heard screaming and groaning as they fell on top of one another, struggling to get back up.

"Oh, this isn't gonna be good," one of the bandits said.

Jerick gave a dark laugh, turning to the man and wrapping his arm around his shoulders. "No, that's where you're wrong. This is going to be a *lot* of fun."

An alarm was sounded as the yelling and screaming of other men behind the wall began to echo through the sky. They were calling out to one another, readying for battle as the alarm continued to ring.

Alaric nodded toward the gate, and they began to walk forward. "Everyone fights," he ordered the people behind him.

Everyone began pulling swords, daggers, staves, and battle axes from their backs or belts, bringing them to a fighting position. In only a few moments, his people were ready to fight. But he knew if things went the way he wanted, it wouldn't require much of a battle.

The gate opened, and men began to pour out. They broke off into large groups as they tried to surround the dark druids. The two bandits in their custody looked around with wild eyes, their breathing heavy as they anticipated the possibility of dying among enemies.

The sound of swords being drawn echoed all around them as Alaric and Jerick stood there, their faces carefree as they looked upon their enemies. As Alaric looked around, he noticed several large dogs alongside their masters. They looked upon them, growling.

"Brother, do you see what I see?" Alaric asked.

Jerick looked just as amused as he nodded, his head rotating as his gaze shifted from one side to the other.

Alaric smiled. "Let's show them the error of their ways."

While Alaric didn't have quite the ability to call on animals that his brother did, it was certainly still there. His eyes flashed, Jerick's following suit. Alaric felt the magic blossoming inside of him, burning through him as he tried to establish connection with the animals.

Slowly, the growling began to wane, and they began to look confused, their masters even more so. The first scream ripped through the air as one of the dogs turned on its master. Several more quickly did the same.

As Alaric and Jerick controlled the animals, Alaric shouted, "Death touch!"

His people rushed forward, their magic not nearly as strong as his. Some of them needed physical contact to use the dark magic, while others had to be within a few feet of their enemy.

He watched with glee as his men and women began to drain the life from many of their soldiers. *Some fight…* It wasn't a fight at all. The enemy stood no chance.

Another barrage of arrows came for them, but a gust of wind blew through, blowing them all off course. Jerick had been paying closer attention than Alaric.

But the plan worked.

"Enough!" a deep voice boomed from the top of the wall.

Alaric's people continued, but he was quick to interject, wanting to greet his new host with sincerity—and threats, if need be.

"Stand down," Alaric ordered.

His people dropped the dark magic, some of their victims falling to the ground on their knees as they gasped for breath, while others struggled to continue standing. Their death touch wasn't nearly the powerful punch Alaric's was, but it did the trick. It scared the enemy soldiers quite a bit, but he knew he had also weakened his people significantly.

It was a price he was willing to pay in order to get what he wanted.

"You wanted to see me?" the man at the top of the wall said.

Alaric took a few steps forward, clasping his hands behind his back as he stood with a confident posture. "If you're Locke, then yes, I did."

The man nodded. "I am. What's this about?"

"I have a bit of a problem that I need to take care of, and I need men to do it. When some of your little friends here stumbled into my camp, I took the opportunity that was presented to me. I forced them to show me the way here, and now I have a request." Alaric stood there, waiting for his response.

"Okay, what is your request?"

Alaric smiled. "We need an army, and you just happen to have one. We also need weapons, a lot of them. My proposition is this… Come fight for me. Come help me take back the Dark Forest, and afterward, I'll help you take the Heights."

Several gasps could be heard, and Alaric knew he had made the impact he wanted to. These men were after amphorald crystals, which were only able to be mined out of the mountains—but the mountains were occupied by the rearick and the mystics.

Alaric had just offered to help them take out their biggest obstacle, allowing them to mine for the gems themselves, without having to steal them and risk the wrath of Arcadia coming down on them.

Several moments passed before the man on top of the wall spoke.

"Why don't you come in? Let's just see what we can do for each other."

CHAPTER TWELVE

Classes had been going well for Amelia, and students seemed to be responding positively to the training. It helped that she taught them meditation first; it had allowed her to teach them more about mental magic without them fatiguing quite so quickly.

She began every class with fifteen minutes of meditation, forcing them to get in the habit of doing so, at least for a short time every day. Even such short sittings would allow them to get better and better at it.

It also allowed them to conserve enough energy to go home and teach their parents or siblings or anyone else close to them.

"All right, everyone," Amelia said. "Today we are going to partner up and take turns learning how to use telepathy. Telepathy is very important. Though it doesn't seem like it would be in comparison to mental shields, in an emergency where stealth is a necessity, being able to communicate without speaking is a blessing."

Amelia asked everyone to pick a partner. There were an odd number of students, so there would be an odd man out. Amelia was happy to alleviate the problem by taking Maddie as her own partner.

Everyone went to work pushing the desks out of the way, so they could sit on the floor. Amelia said she concentrated best when she sat in the lotus position, so she instructed everyone else to do the same.

"Though touch isn't necessary for telepathy, or any other mental magic, for that matter, in the beginning, it might help you establish a connection. Reach out and hold hands with your partner," she instructed.

Everyone followed her instructions, including Maddie. Without being told, every student in the classroom closed their eyes and began to focus.

Amelia faced Maddie as though she were speaking to her directly, but continued to direct everyone in the room. "Relax your shoulders and relax your body. Take several slow, deep breaths. Focus on the person sitting in front of you. When you begin to call on your magic, your body will become aware of the minds of others. You might not be able to hear them, but you'll be able to feel them."

Following her own teaching, Amelia relaxed her shoulders and her body to demonstrate. Her eyes flashed white, and she focused on the students around her. Across from her, Maddie seemed to be focusing, but not really getting anywhere.

"If you're having trouble, focus on yourself first. Once you've centered yourself, you'll be able to focus on someone else," Amelia told them.

She could almost feel the relief of several other students, and she knew it was because they, too, were having trouble. After several minutes, Amelia could feel some of the students making a light connection with one another; she could even feel the light tickle of Maddie brushing against her mind.

Amelia let down some of her own barrier, allowing Maddie to communicate with her.

…not even working. I'm terrible at this.

Amelia almost laughed at the girl for her irritation. She only caught the tail end of that, but it seemed Maddie hadn't yet figured out she had successfully connected with Amelia.

Try not to focus so hard, Amelia said telepathically.

Maddie jumped a little, a hesitant smile turning a corner of her mouth. *Was this me? Or did you just make the connection yourself?*

Amelia smiled. *This was all you. I just let you in.*

Looking around the room, Amelia asked, "Who has made their first connections?" Everyone in the room raised their hand, including Maddie. "Good! Now break the connection and try again."

"Amelia?" Salazar, one of her students, said lightly.

She turned to face him. "Yes?"

"I know this stuff is important, and I'm very happy to learn— especially after everything we've been through. But my dad is a guard, and I talked to some of the other guys that are in the self-defense courses. I'd like to join," he said.

Brady, a Boulevard student sitting a few feet from him, nodded. "I'm not the fighting type. I've always been tall and skinny, and not very strong, but I still want to help guard the city. I can throw really hot fireballs, and I'm a fast learner. What do you think about having a magical division of the guard?"

Amelia sighed as she sat there, her eyes unfocused as she thought over his proposition. "In the past, the Hunters knew magic. A lot of the guards did, too, but it was mainly reserved for the Hunters. The best of the best. That being said, I've seen what magic users can do on top of the wall, and it's obvious we need a range of warriors."

He smiled. "Is that a yes?"

She laughed. "It's a 'maybe'. I think your idea is a very good one, but until you guys know how to properly protect yourselves, I'm not going to risk your lives on the wall. If you can prove to me that you can create an acceptable mental shield, as well as an acceptable physical magic shield, I'll consider it."

Turning to Salazar, she smiled. "As for you, same rules apply. You have to show me you can create a mental barrier. If you guys train in here with me, and keep up, then I'll be happy to consider training you in other areas as well."

Salazar narrowed his eyes and winked. *You're on*, he sent telepathically.

She rather liked his forwardness. The students wanted to protect themselves as well as protect their families; if she could help drive them to do that, she would do whatever it took.

<hr>

IT HAD BEEN RAINING for most of the morning, and smells in the Dark Forest had come alive. Corrine always loved the smell of the Terres Forest, but the Dark Forest smelled a thousand times better. The leaves and flowers there were much more aromatic, and they filled the senses and relaxed the body.

It was the Chieftain's turn to go out hunting, and Corrine asked if she could accompany him. She wanted to take another shot at it.

It had broken her heart, knowing that, last time, she had hurt the deer by trying to push her influence on the animal and force it into submission. Corrine hadn't had enough practice to have that kind of power, though, so all she had done was piss the deer off and hurt it. She had more than learned her lesson, though, and she wanted to do it right this time.

As always, the Chieftain was overjoyed to have the little girl with him. Corrine loved that he compared her often to Arryn, and loved the idea she could be good like them.

Since coming to the Dark Forest, she had been accepted and adopted in ways she never thought possible. For the first time in her life, she had a family, and she would stop at nothing to make them proud of her.

It was Corinne's idea to bring Christopher along, wanting him to get out of the village and experience a little bit of freedom. Even as young as she was, she knew he had been cooped up for too long. Wandering always did her good, especially when her mind was full. She wanted him to give it a shot, and see if it helped.

"So, when I approach an animal, the magic is similar to healing magic, right?" Corrine asked.

Her mistake last time was that she had pushed her influence on the animal, forcing it into submission. That approach always caused intense pain for the animal, but once it submitted, the power could be lifted, creating a subservient animal while no longer causing it pain.

"Allow your magic to grow, and focus on the animal with the best of intentions. The magic will draw them to you, even without you pushing any toward them. The animals of the Dark Forest are naturally curious about us, so you shouldn't have to use much effort. When you do use your magic, focus on the animal as you would if you were about to heal them. The magic feels similar, but it is different. I'll guide you once we get to that point," he said.

It sounded complicated, but Corrine had faith that the Chieftain wouldn't let her down. She knew he would help her through it.

Corrine heard something off in the distance, and she opened herself up. Her eyes flashed green as she began to search the area. Soon, she felt several life forces not too far away, but they felt very small.

Without warning, she broke into a run, the Chieftain and Christopher calling for her to come back. Before long, she could hear whimpers and whines. Reaching out, she could even feel fear, and she wondered what she was about to find.

She rounded a large rock, and her eyes widened as she saw a large wolf lying dead on the ground. Surrounding her were six small wolf pups. Corrine's jaw dropped as she rushed over, knelt next to them, and reached out to touch them.

They were very sick, and one, the seventh pup, had already passed. They weren't more than a day old, and she wasn't sure how they had survived for that long.

"Corrine, are you okay?" the Chieftain asked as he, too, rounded the rock.

In her arms were two tiny wolf pups, their eyes still closed as they whimpered against her, nuzzling her as they searched for milk. She looked up at the Chieftain with wide, bright green eyes.

"They're all alone," she said.

The Chieftain and Christopher both looked at her with sadness on their faces as they knelt next to her. The Chieftain pointed to the mother. "There is a lot of blood behind her; far too much to be normal for birth. It seems she suffered complications, and bled out."

"There are lots of wolves in the villages," Christopher said. "Have any recently had pups?"

The Chieftain thought for a moment before nodding. "I don't think there are any directly in the village, but I do know of one wolf inside the barrier who has had pups recently."

Corrine's face lit up. "We have to take them with us! They'll die without our help!"

The Chieftain nodded. "No worries, little one. We'll take the pups with us, and the mother, too. We'll see to it that she's cremated, and her ashes are scattered. She died bringing life into this world, and she deserves a ceremony."

Corrine giggled as the little black wolf pup in her hand nuzzled up to her neck and began licking her. "You won't find milk there, little one, but we'll find you some soon."

The Chieftain placed a hand on Christopher's shoulder. "Those pups need milk right away; they have nearly reached their limit. If you would, please escort Corrine back to the village. Elysia should be able to help locate the mother wolf. She will keep them safe."

The tiny black wolf in her hand continued to root around her neck, grunting and whining as he did so. The others seemed to be very lethargic.

"That one right there is a fighter," Christopher observed as he removed his shirt and began wrapping the pups in it.

Corrine nodded and smiled as she laid her head gently down on the wolf's. "Yes, he is. I'm gonna keep him. I think I'll name him Reaper."

Christopher shared a look with the Chieftain before turning back to Corrine. "Reaper? His mother *did* die while giving birth to him, you realize."

She shrugged. "And he's the strongest out of all of them. He's also the biggest. When he's full-grown, I have no doubt he'll be powerful. He deserves a strong name. Besides, if you were dying, and someone gave you a strong name, wouldn't it make you want to fight even harder? Or should I call him Fluffy? Would you fight to live for a name like Fluffy?"

Christopher opened his mouth and then closed it again, unsure of what to say. He was stunned by the logic.

"Reaper it is," the Chieftain said. "I can't say I can argue her points. Perhaps we should name them all."

Corrine walked away, smiling as she cradled the little boy up to her chest, her pinky in his mouth to soothe him.

CHAPTER THIRTEEN

Leaving Roger wasn't nearly as emotional this time as it was the last. Arryn knew she would see him again, and she knew the Dark Forest would be better for it. By the time they left, their entire cart had been filled with strong, impressive weapons. She wasn't sure if there would be enough, but there was certainly plenty to get them through the upcoming battle.

They simply didn't have the time to stay with Roger any longer.

As they moved south, Arryn stopped in at the farmhouse, wanting to visit the old woman. The farmland looked wonderful, and seemed to be thriving in only the short amount of time since they had left.

Roger hadn't taken much out of the bag of coins, which Arryn still felt guilty for, but she also felt guilty for spending someone else's money. In the end, she felt it was a fair trade. Every one of them was too goodhearted to take from another, so only a small amount was taken.

The old woman almost seemed offended that Arryn hadn't taken more, but when she spied the massive cart full of weapons, she realized she had just got a good deal on the steel.

Though her son was gone forever, Elsie took solace in knowing that his killers would never take anyone else from their loved ones ever again. Arryn had seen to that.

Instead of cutting to the west, Arryn and Cathillian continued to ride south.

Arryn had a mission of her own. Ever since her father had been back in the Dark Forest, she had wanted to retrieve something of his, something he had long forgotten.

Well, until recently that is.

Shortly after her own arrival in Arcadia, she had wandered the city until she found her childhood home, which had been preserved just the way it was the night they had left.

That had all been Celine's doing, of course, but it was incredible all the same. Behind the front door, Christopher had always kept his three most favorite swords, ready if he ever had need of them.

That of course, had been good placement for them if he had been answering the door, but if a group of power-hungry, evil, horrible Hunters broke into your house in the middle of the night to assassinate your family, well, it would have been good to have them located in other places as well.

All the same, Arryn planned to retrieve them.

She couldn't wait to see the look on her father's face when she handed them over.

As they came to the city gates, four guards stepped out and greeted her. Two of them were guards that she and Cathillian had trained themselves. Their faces lit up as they stepped forward, and they placed an arm over their chests, saluting in the druid way.

Arryn felt honored that they would remember and show such respect to her, especially after everything that had happened.

"Arryn!" Danny said. "What are the two of you doing here?"

She smiled and pointed to the wall. "I see we still haven't learned our lesson, now have we? No archers?"

Danny shook his head and smiled, looking at her with an amused expression. "Hey, now… Don't give us too hard of a time. A lot has happened, but all good things. We have a lot of trained men now, and Amelia is working on getting ranged fighters on the wall. Mostly magic, though, I think. That's what she says whenever students bring it up, or she speaks to us about it."

Arryn laughed. "All right, then. I guess I won't give you too much shit. Did you say Amelia has students?"

He nodded. "As the only mental magic user in the city, she's teaching a mental magic defense course at the Academy. She has also initiated self-defense courses for adults as well. Absolutely anyone with the will to learn is now able to attend. As long as they give back to the city in some way, their tuition is forgiven."

Arryn looked over to Cathillian, and he smiled. She did as well. "It seems she learned quite a lot in the Dark Forest," Arryn said.

Danny nodded. "She's the same. She works just as hard for us as she always has, but she's different, too. Whatever she experienced out in the woods with you guys definitely affected her."

"So, do you guys need to pat me down and frisk me? Or can I go inside?" she asked.

Danny laughed. "Are you asking, or offering? Because if you're asking, feel free to go inside. If you feel like you need a good frisking, I'm your man."

Cathillian cleared his throat. "That depends on if you want to keep your hands and face or not."

Still smiling, Danny looked over to Cathillian and said, "You know I love you, man. But, I have to say, I'm way more afraid of her than I am of you."

Cathillian raised his left brow. "Who did you think I was talking about?"

They all laughed, and Danny took a few steps back, waving them through. "Welcome back to the city, Arryn and Cathillian."

The druids waived to their friends as they made their way

inside. Arryn was surprised to see the trees still stood and looking over at Cathillian, it seemed he was just as surprised.

The cobblestone road had been rebuilt around them—now there was an adequate circle of space around each tree that would allow them to grow and expand even further. The road wound outward a little around each one, only to come back in, and then round out again at the next tree. It was beautiful. The way it was set up, it looked as though you could do figure eights around the trees.

Arryn loved it.

As they traveled through the streets, she smiled at how different things were. When she had been in the city before, she had seen children playing together, and the men and women working together, but she could sense the tension.

Now as she traveled through, she saw the beautiful gowns on the little noble girls, right alongside the clean, but cheaply-made dresses the Boulevard girls wore. They all ran around the street together, kicking a ball back and forth, not a care in the world. It wasn't at all tense as it had been before.

Off in the distance, Arryn could see the Academy, and she looked over to Cathillian. "I had plans to go straight to the house, and then maybe stop at the Capitol building before leaving, but I think I'd like to stop in at the Academy. What do you say?"

He only smiled and nodded, and she knew he would have agreed to anything she asked. For the most part, that was just how he was with her. Without a doubt, she knew he would follow her to the ends of the earth if she had need of him.

They made it to the Academy, and dismounted. Cathillian asked Chaos to stay outside, but Snow followed Arryn inside. As soon as they crossed the threshold, the familiar smells hit Arryn.

She could also smell the fresh wood and paint, even from the main floor. "They must be redoing that room I blew apart. That little rat bastard still pisses me off when I think of him."

Cathillian laughed. "Consider me shocked. Just don't look at my face, because you'll see I'm a lying asshole."

She laughed as she led him up the stairs. Turning right would take them toward what had once been Talia's office, and left would lead them toward the classrooms. They headed down the classroom hallway, and Arryn could hear grunts and sounds of fighting underneath them. It traveled through the halls on the bottom floor.

She began to worry, but then she heard a loud, "Stop!" and she knew it was a training class.

"Good for them," Cathillian said. "I really think she did take a lot from the Dark Forest. I can sense children and early teens down there."

Arryn's magic was strong, but she didn't have the ability to tell someone's age by their life force. Only a general sense of old or young.

As they walked down the hall, they peeked into windows, fully aware they looked like creeps. They had made it all the way down to the end, but hadn't quite reached the door yet when it blew open, and Amelia ran into the hall with a big smile on her face.

"Arryn!" she said before coming over and wrapping her in a hug. "I thought I sensed you!"

Arryn looked suspiciously at the former Chancellor turned governor. "Were you just looking in my head? If so, you've gotten really good at it, because I didn't even feel you rooting around in there."

Amelia laughed and shook her head. "Not at all. I'm teaching a mental magic class, and it requires all of us to have a very open mind. I've been in your head more than a few times, so I just sensed you coming. I didn't believe it at first, but I guess I was right. Come inside! You have to see the students."

Arryn hesitated for a moment, remembering just how hated she was the last time she had been in a classroom. Talia and Scarlett had been working nonstop to brainwash the students into hating her.

After a few moment's hesitation, Arryn finally acquiesced, following Amelia into the classroom.

As soon as she crossed the threshold, faces all over began to light up as students jumped up off the floor and crowded around her. Arryn's eyes were wide, and she looked around in obvious shock.

"Well, I certainly didn't expect this!" she said with a nervous smile.

"We've missed you!" Maddie said. "It might have been rough there for a while, but everyone here knows what you did; everyone knows they wouldn't have their free will, and maybe their lives, if it weren't for you."

There were several nods and cheers of agreement from the students, each of them struggling to get closer to her to shake her hand and thank her for what she had done for them.

"You save the city over and over, and if it weren't for you, I don't think my mom and dad would have the opportunity to take self-defense courses at night. I don't think my older brother, who was too old to attend the Academy, would be able to take night classes to learn magic," one of the students, a young woman about Maddie's age, told her.

Another student stepped forward. "Yeah, and if it weren't for you, I wouldn't be training in magic in here during the day, and combat training at night. I want to be a guard. I want to help defend the city."

Over and over, students shared their stories about how Arryn had changed their lives, and it was all she could do to hold back tears. She had never been so overwhelmed with gratitude before.

For a moment, her mind wandered. *If my dad could only see this now.* But then even more happiness radiated through her as she remembered all she had to do was go back to the Dark Forest, and she could tell him herself.

Everything her parents had ever wanted for her: strength, confidence, dedication, she had it all, and it allowed her not only to save lives, but to enrich them.

While she despised losing her parents the way that she did, she was aware that her pain was nothing in the grand scheme of things. Everything she had gone through was for a greater purpose—one she was happy to be part of.

Once everyone had said their piece, Amelia dismissed the class early and instructed them to continue practicing telepathy and meditation with a partner. They walked outside into the hall, and allowed the students to clear before speaking.

"Well, what did you think about that?" Amelia asked, smiling.

Arryn's eyes were still wide as she fell silent, shaking her head.

"Stunned to silence," Cathillian said. "Damn, I need to bring her here more often."

Arryn shot him a dirty look and reached out to punch him in the arm. It completely knocked him off balance, and he stumbled a couple feet, rubbing his arm in an exaggerated fashion.

"Ouch! How rude!" he said, then smiling. She knew he was faking.

She rolled her eyes and shook her head again. "You want to keep him? I'll sell him to you for cheap. In fact, you can just have him."

Amelia just laughed at the two of them. "I have missed the two of you. How have you been? Oh! Did the twins ever find you?"

"They are kind of intense," Arryn said.

Amelia snorted. "You haven't seen them fight yet." She paused then looked at her with curiosity. "Or have you? Have you fought the dark druids yet?"

"Not yet, but we will soon. We went north to find a blacksmith that Arryn had met on her way home from the Frozen North. We needed weapons badly," Cathillian said.

"Are the twins really that impressive?" Arryn asked.

"I'm surprised I didn't die when I saw Bast do her thing; I have no doubt she's capable of a lot more. I don't know a lot about the places outside of the Arcadian Valley, but I know the world is still in ruin, even now. There are very few places where communities and civilizations have been able to thrive. Kemet is their home, but it's mostly desert. They would have to be extremely hard-working people to survive there," Amelia said.

Arryn gave a devious smile. "I have to admit, I'm pretty curious to see what they're capable of. I would challenge them to a sparring match, but after they told me how they channel their magic through their fists and feet to give them bone shattering hits, I don't really feel that would be a very good idea."

Amelia shook her head, and mouthed the word 'no' in an exaggerated motion. "Absolutely not. I took back one of the bodies because I was curious to see exactly how much damage she had done. I had the medical examiner do an autopsy, and with the amount of strength she hit him with, it damn near lique-fied his insides, and his spine was dust. I have a man in the cells who survived being punched in the back by her, and I have no idea how he did it. Fucking lucky is all I can say."

"Holy Bitch!" Arryn said. "Sounds to me like the matriarch blessed her—" she paused, obviously waiting for something as a large smile spread.

Cathillian sighed and shook his head. "Arryn… Are you serious? Don't you dare say it."

"*Hand over fist,*" Arryn said before busting out laughing. "Huh, huh? See what I did there?"

Amelia snorted as Cathillian just shook his head in exasperation.

Arryn laughed again. "He hates it *so* much when I do that! It makes it so much funnier."

"It's not that I hate it, it's just so ridiculous that I can't even process it," he said.

She shrugged. "Well, *I* find me hilarious. Anyway, no war yet on our side. The twins have settled in nicely, and they have acclimated pretty quickly, especially given where they came from. I imagine it would be quite a shock going from completely desert-ridden area to the forest, but they are managing just fine. Dante is growing like a weed. Like a magically grown weed. When we left, he was the size of a large medium-sized dog. I'm curious to see what he looks like now. How about you? How are things here?"

"Things are good. Marie will be taking over my place soon, and I have been transitioning to the position of governor. The Academy has grown exponentially, and classes go from sunup to well after sundown; kids during the day, adults at night. There have been a rash of bandit attacks down south, and they have been trickling closer and closer to Arcadia, but from what I've found out from my friend in the dungeon, they have no plan of approaching Arcadia directly."

"Oh, we know all about those bandits," Arryn said with a smile. "We killed a few on our way up north. Seems there is an entire group of them south of the Heights. I figure once the Dark Forest is secure, we can head down there and find out what the hell is going on. Besides, it'll be on our way. We promised our assistance to Bast and Cleo because they are offering theirs."

Amelia let go a sigh of contentment. "I'd be lying if I said that wasn't a relief. I haven't learned too much, but from what I have, it seemed like that was going to be quite a difficult task. I hate to ask you to do something like that, but if I'm to be honest, I trust you to do a better job of it than what the guards could. I've seen what you can do. Like the Queen Bitch herself, I'm pretty sure you're unkillable."

Arryn laughed. "Don't let *Her* hear that. She'll come down and kill us all in our sleep. Besides, I've nearly died a few times. Speaking of which, the last time I nearly died, I managed to rescue my father."

Amelia's eyes widened as her hands went to cover her mouth. "You did? That's fantastic! I'm so happy you found him."

Arryn went on to tell the story of how she found her father.

How they had lost several people in the attack with the dark druids, and the methods those bastards had used to get the best of them. Amelia stood there in shock and disgust as she listened to the story.

"I'm sorry to hear all that, but from the sound of it, it'll all be over soon. I know you probably don't, but do you have time to hang out for a little while? Catch up?"

Arryn smiled and shook her head. "Unfortunately, we don't. We need to get back to the Dark Forest. I wanted to stop by the city and pick up a couple things from my old house. My father had swords, and I wanted to stop by Girard's and see if my mother's painting is still there."

"No worries," Amelia said. "The houses are both as you left them."

They hugged one another and said their goodbyes. Arryn took one last look at the Academy on her way out, wondering if she would ever be there again.

CHAPTER FOURTEEN

Alaric and Jerick had been in the mercenary camp for a while, and it seemed that their discussions were finally coming to a close. The two Chieftains had been left alone with their people, while Locke and his men discussed potentially working with the dark druids.

Alaric wasn't a very patient man, and his brother, Jerick, was even less so. They had nearly lost what little they had left when Locke returned with an answer.

"Good evening, gentlemen," Locke said, his deep voice booming inside of the large tent as he came in and sat at a table. "Sorry for the wait."

Alaric lifted a brow as he stared him down. "Yes, it was certainly quite the wait. We've been here for a couple days now, and we are running out of time."

Jerick nodded his head. "We hope you've come to a conclusion, yes?"

Locke stroked his thick, dark beard as he leaned back in the chair, dramatically pausing as he looked from one man to the other. "We have a counter offer."

Jerick began to stand, but Alaric grabbed his arm to still him. "What might that be?" Jerick asked through gritted teeth.

"You want us to help you take the Dark Forest back. We've heard stories about the druids our entire lives, and meeting you, I'd have to say I believe every one of them. That being said, if you're coming to us, that means you're not the biggest or the baddest. If you need help, the druids you face are even stronger. That means we are risking our necks and getting nothing in return."

Alaric nodded his head. "More or less, though I already offered to help take the Heights for you. That's not exactly *nothing*, though I can see why that would be a concern for you. So, what is it you want?"

A young woman walked into the tent, her eyes downcast to the ground. She was in little more than a leather bra and leather shorts that the dark Chieftain wasn't even certain would cover anything if she were to bend over. From what he had seen, this was how most of the women in the community dressed, even those as young as sixteen.

The young woman handed Locke a beer and slightly bowed her head, careful never to look them in the eye. She began to turn, and he reached out, grabbing her wrist and spinning her around to sit on his lap.

He gave a rather disgusting smile as he stared at the girl. "What do I want?"

Jerick growled as he shook his head. "You. Not your dick. What the fuck do you want from us in return for your service?"

Locke laughed as he pushed the girl off his lap. She fell to the ground, landing on her knees and momentarily looking up, before he roughly lifted his flattened hand. Fearing the strike that she knew would soon come, she quickly looked back down to the ground and scurried out of the tent as quickly as possible.

"Hmm, well, we have a fight of our own. The Heights contains the mines that are full of exactly what we need: amphorald crystals. We need all of those that we can get. The problem is the rearick. Short, stocky little bastards, but they can fight. We are ex-Hunters and ex-Arcadian Guard, but they are pretty powerful. Certainly, not to be underestimated."

Jerick sighed, and Alaric was quick to reach out again, hoping to still him. "And you want us to help you, what? Take the Heights? Because as we've said, we already agreed to that."

Locke took a long drink from his beer, a stream flowing from each corner of his mouth and down his beard. He set it down on the table hard, the liquid sloshing around and several drops spilling out onto the table.

"I want those little fuckers dead. We only need a couple dozen of them. We put them in chains and force them to do the digging. That's all we need. The problem is we not only have to take Craigston to make this happen, we need to take the Temple, as well. If those mind fuckers get even a whiff of what we're planning, they will come down, and that will be a hell none of us want to face. Physical magic is good, but if you can weaken them from a distance like you did with my men, you're exactly what we need."

Alaric and Jerick both smiled as they looked at one another. "Tell me," Jerick said. "Have you ever heard of Manchineel?"

Locke looked at him with confusion. Shaking his head, he said, "No, I can't say that I have."

Jerick began to tell him all about the plant and what the smoke could do. With their training, if they could sneak around the Temple without being heard, and get close enough without being within range for the mental magicians to get into their heads, they could set the fires and blow the smoke into the Temple. Unlike the druids, the smoke would kill them; there would be no saving themselves.

They would choke on their own blood, their lungs filling with it as they suffocated.

"I like the way you think," Locke said. "I think you have yourself a deal. From the sound of it, we can take the Heights with ease. The problem is, we can't use that smoke on the rearick. If we do, we'll kill them all, and we still need a few to do the mining."

Alaric waved a hand. "No worries. We have plenty of ways to take them out. So, we have a deal? You help us take the Dark Forest, we grow the plants that you need and teach you how to use them without injuring yourselves in the process. Then we will help you take the Heights in return."

Locke nodded his head, reaching his hand out. Alaric stood and accepted it, shaking as they made their agreement.

"Good," Alaric said. "Now, show me these magitech weapons I've been hearing so much about. Maybe it's time we modernize ourselves a little, at least for the battle to come."

SVEN HAD JUST WOKEN UP, ready to get a start on the day. He would be heading back to Arcadia with his brother on a gem run. The rearick had been changing up their patterns to confuse the bandits, but it seemed they were wising up to it.

They had planned to leave much earlier, but had been forced to stay as Tavich wasn't too excited to let anyone leave Craigston for any reason and wanted to wait on those that were out to return.

The brothers had discussed talking to Amelia, but hadn't yet been able to make the trip. She seemed like a pretty alright woman, and according to his brother, Ren, she was more than all right. She was a fighter. He couldn't help but respect a strong woman, especially a pretty one like that.

As soon as he walked outside, he could smell the fresh morning air. The dew was still settled on the grass, and a little fog had settled on his lake. He went out to his barn and readied one of his horses, a good girl named Sadie; his most trusted one.

After packing everything he needed, he climbed onto Sadie's back and took off toward town. He was just far enough away that he didn't have to listen to the drunkards stumbling around, but close enough that he could get there quickly.

As expected, his brother was already at Ophelia's, brew in hand, waiting for him.

"It's about time. I never thought ye'd show."

Sven rolled his eyes as he dismounted. He walked up and punched his brother in the arm, stealing the beer right out of his hand. "The sun ain't even all the way up yet, ye lard. Quit givin' me shite."

Ren went for the beer, but Sven quickly drained it.

"Thanks. I needed that ta deal with yer petty shite this morn," Sven said.

Ren punched his brother in the face, the action fast enough that the older rearick didn't have a chance to prepare for it. He unleashed a laugh, twisting his jaw back and forth before closing his mouth again.

"Pretty sure ye hit harder as a newborn babe. Little brother, ye wouldn't be goin' and gettin' soft on me, now would ye?"

Ren growled for a moment before his scowl faded and he, too, broke into laughter. "Yer about a right twat this mornin', ain't ye? What crawled into yer panties an' got 'em into a bunch?"

Sven was about to answer when shouts broke out. "What is that? What's happenin'?"

Ren looked ahead, his brows furrowing as he shook his head. "They're rushin' through with a cart. That must be the crew ol' Tavich was a waitin' on."

Sven's eyes closed for a moment, his fists tightening at his sides. "Fuck me."

Nodding, Ren said, "Yeah. If I was a bettin' man, an' we both know that I am, I'd have ta say that cart is full o' dead an' injured."

Sven didn't say another word before walking back and quickly mounting his horse again. He kicked at her sides, and she took off with a start. They caught up with the cart in only a matter of moments.

"What happened here?" Sven asked, though he already knew.

"Those damn bandits!" Randy, one of the men helping get them into the medical building, said. "They got us again! We fought most of 'em off, killed quite a few. The rest scattered, but we lost a few of 'r own. Somethin' needs ta be done."

The sound of horses trampling through caught Sven's attention, and he turned to see his brother ride up.

"Well?" Ren asked.

"Just how well do ye know Amelia?" Sven asked, irritation in his voice.

Ren shrugged. "Well enough, I'd say. She's a good lass. What did ye have in mind?"

Sven's nostrils were flaring with every breath he took. He felt rage at how much loss their people had seen from the greed of the bandits. It didn't seem to matter how many they killed; there were more coming all the time, and they had no idea where they were coming from.

"I'm gonna go talk ta Tavich. No work today," Sven said. "In fact, there won't be any more work at all. Not until this gets settled. I'll make sure of it."

Sven turned to several men that were running up, one of which was the foreman at the mine. "Hey! Will," Sven said.

The man he called Will stopped, his red beard blowing in the wind. "What is it? I need ta see ta the men. I need ta make sure they're gonna be all right. I'm hopin' I don't have ta make another stop ta talk ta widows."

Sven shook his head. "From what I was just told, there are a couple that died, a few more injured. Listen, I know we all need the coin, but not this bad. From now until further notice, until I find out what the feck is goin' on around here, the mines're shut down. If I catch any of ye in there, I'll rip yer heads off meself. We don't need any more widows. I'm goin' to Arcadia ta settle this.

We don't know where these bandits are comin' from, but it's just as much Arcadia's problem as it is ours. The only difference is *they* have an army."

"Amelia will help us if we ask," Ren said. "She's strong, and she serves justice. She's not gonna let this go."

Sven snorted. "Well, it's been goin' on fer this long. That stunt we pulled against the bandit group with Amelia and the earthmover was a good show, but it's still carryin' on. We need ta stop this now. We need ta find out where it's comin' from and put 'n end to it."

"I'll do what I can here," Will said. "You get ta Arcadia an' get us the help we need."

Once again, without saying a word, Sven squeezed Sadie's sides, and she took off. It wasn't safe for only him and his brother to travel the road to Arcadia, but the way he felt right then, it would take the Matriarch and the Patriarch to save the souls of anyone who dared try to stop them, and he knew damn well neither one of them would stand in his way.

CHAPTER FIFTEEN

Being back in her old house, and even visiting Girard's house again, was quite emotional for Arryn. In the end, instead of taking her mother's painting back with her, she decided to give it to Amelia for safe keeping. Amelia had promised to hide it in a place where it couldn't be damaged, and no one would find it, bringing peace to Arryn's mind.

She had wanted to bring it back with her to the Dark Forest, but she didn't want to risk the dark druids attacking and something terrible happening. At the same time, she didn't want to leave it in Girard's house or her childhood home for fear of someone breaking in and destroying the home or their possessions.

The swords, however, were another story. She retrieved all three from behind the door in her childhood home, excited to get them back to her father.

Riding into the Dark Forest, she and Cathillian looked at one another with curiosity as they saw a massive stone wall surrounding the southeast corner of the druid territory. It seemed to expand one hundred feet or so in each direction.

"Well, that's both new and interesting," Arryn said as she looked it over.

Cathillian nodded. "Apparently, the twins have been very busy."

The two made their way inside, heading for the village. When they got there, Elysia ran out to greet them, a broad smile on her face.

"You're back! How was the trip?" Elysia asked.

"Eh, it was pretty good. I tried to sell your son to Amelia, but she didn't want him. Maybe next time, though," Arryn said.

Elysia looked at her with furrowed brows. "Exactly how hard did you try?"

"Mother!" Cathillian scolded. "I'm your baby boy. How dare you? You know you would die without my adorable face to greet you every day."

Elysia laughed. "If that's what you think, then sure, Son." She turned to Arryn and whispered loudly, "Next time, take me with you. We'll get a great deal, and they'll actually take him."

Cathillian shook his head, making a *tsk*ing noise. "Sometimes I just don't know about the two of you."

Arryn smiled and gave him a wink. She dismounted as she saw her father walking around the fire. He was wearing druid clothing and had a smile on his face. He looked genuinely happy.

"How has he been doing?" Arryn asked.

Elysia turned to follow her gaze and saw Christopher leaning over to take something that Corrine was handing him. He smiled as the little girl reached up and wrapped her arms around his neck. He wrapped his own arms around her, hugging her tight before releasing her.

"He's adjusting nicely," Elysia said. "It was rough at first. While you were gone, he was having bad dreams again. Zoe and I worked our magic, and he seems to be benefiting greatly. The nightmares have almost disappeared completely."

She smiled and nodded. "That makes me so happy to hear. I was worried what would happen while I was—"

There was a loud growl, and Arryn was tackled to the ground.

She twisted her face from side to side, her eyes closed tight, and her expression scrunched up as she tried to protect herself from the attack of incessant licking. She gave a hard shove, and Dante backed off. As she wiped her face, she was finally able to open her eyes, and they widened further.

"What the hell?" she finally managed.

The white tiger, which up until the week before had been a cub, stepped forward and gave her a headbutt, rubbing his cheek against her. The surprise came from just how far down he had to bend in order to do so. Looking at him now, he seemed to be nearly the size his mother was when she first found them. She would estimate him at only around a hundred pounds lighter than she had been at that time, but that was it. And in tiger terms, one hundred pounds was not a lot.

"What happened to you?" Arryn asked with a smile as she reached up and scratched his face.

She could feel him almost beaming through their bond. He was so happy and so proud, and the fact that he was able to sneak up on her and take her down to the ground without anyone noticing him made him even happier. He was a proud big-little boy, and she made sure to send her love and happiness right back through the bond to him.

"Big boy! You're almost big enough for Corrine to ride now. Actually, you may already be. If you keep growing like this, I'll have to alternate trips between the two of you," she said.

Snow came over and nuzzled Dante's face with her own. She purred and groaned with love as she continued to snuggle him, and then started to bathe his face.

Arryn heard a squeaking sound. Turning, she went to the cart and flung back the tarp that protected the newly forged swords from the elements. Each was tied together and secured to the cart, so they didn't move. In the very corner of the cart was a topless, solid oak box. Arryn placed her hands inside and pulled free a snow-white rabbit.

"Well, who's this? Don't tell me you have a third familiar," Elysia said with wide eyes. Arryn thought that she was joking until she turned and saw the expression on her face.

It was unheard of for a druid to have more than one familiar unless their previous one had died, but Arryn had two. Elysia obviously didn't doubt her ability to possibly have three.

Arryn laughed. "No, no. Though, we did build quite a bond on the mountain. This is Wiggles Von Puffybritches."

Elysia looked at her with obvious confusion. "Did you just say…"

Cathillian nodded in an exaggerated fashion. "Yes. Yes, she did. And let me just say, that is a different name than she has given the last five people who've asked."

Dante stepped forward and sniffed the rabbit before giving him a lick. She could feel the recognition coming through the bond. He recognized the rabbit and even wanted to play with him. Suddenly, Arryn felt terrible for the tiger cub. He might have the body of a full-grown predator, but he was still a baby at heart.

Christopher wandered over, all smiles as he locked eyes on his daughter. "You're back! I'm so happy to see both of you safe. Who's your friend?"

Elysia and Cathillian both laughed. Cathillian held out his hand. "Yes, Arryn, do tell him. Who's your friend?"

"Oh, well, I'm so glad you asked. This is Whiskers Hopskitoosh."

Cathillian looked at her with nothing shy of shock on his face. "*Hopskitoosh*? You can't be serious. Now, I *know* you're screwing with us."

She cradled the rabbit even closer. "Twitchy Jigglybum, don't you dare let him make you feel bad about your names."

Cathillian threw his arms in the air with exasperation. "I don't know how you do it. It took me *days* to come up with a name for Echo, and I chose it because her screams 'echo' through the woods. That's the equivalent of my grandfather choosing to name Zobig 'Grumbles'. Here *you* are, naming every animal you find something new, and they all have a hundred different names each."

She shrugged. "I'm just talented, I guess. Don't be jealous. Also, I call him Grumbles all the time. He's a very grumpy beast."

Arryn handed the rabbit over to her father, watching the smile spread across his face as he gently rubbed his ears.

"Aw, you're such a cute little thing, aren't you, Higglebottom Whiskerface?" Christopher said.

Arryn laughed. "Ha! That must be where I get it from!"

Christopher laughed as he focused back in on the rabbit. "You got your looks from your mama, but you got your wit from your daddy."

"Then which one of you is it that carried the gene that was destined to hate me and pick on me all the time?" Cathillian asked.

With another laugh, Christopher said, "Well, I would say that's probably me, too. I just haven't gotten to know you very well yet. But there's time."

Cathillian waved his hands in the air with sarcasm. "*Yay.*" He quirked a smile at the man.

Arryn walked to the cart and grabbed a bundle of swords that had been separated from the rest. She carried them over to her father and extended her hands. "Look what I found."

His eyes widened as he looked from the swords to his daughter. "Seriously? Where did you find these?"

Arryn smiled. "After we fled, and I guess after you were captured, Celine watched the house, taking care of it and making sure nothing happened to it. As a result, everything inside is almost exactly the same. Even mom's painting of all of us was still there. It's not now; I had it taken out, in case anyone decided to go in there. Once Celine was gone, there wasn't anyone to watch it, and there were break-ins by Adrien's horrible daughter Talia. She killed a couple people there—at least one that I know of—so I didn't want to risk anyone harming it. Anyway, I figured you might want these back."

He sat the rabbit down on the ground, giving him one last scratch before standing and accepting the gift. Each sword was of a different style, and was used for a different style of fighting. They were modeled after some of the battle swords the new ancients, and even some of the old ancients, had used.

One was a katana; his favorite. Her mother had commissioned it specifically for him after a friend of his found an actual relic on a dig in a mine. Well, he had purchased it for quite a lot of money from the rearick who had found it.

"Thank you, Arryn. This means the world to me. Just having something personal from my old life in my hands again is indescribable. It reminds me of my life with you and your mother before anything bad happened."

She smiled, taking a step forward and wrapping her arms around him. "Tell me, have you thought about training?"

She stepped away to judge his expression, and was surprised to see a spark that hadn't been there before. He used to be a great swordsman, and she knew he could be again, with a little work.

"Only if I can train with you," he said.

She smiled. "I thought you'd never ask."

They turned and began to walk back toward the village. Snow helped Arryn and Chaos with the cart, and then Cathillian helped her unload everything and gather the warriors to show them what they had received.

Once everything was settled and the weapons were all put away and ready for when they would need them, the group gathered in around the fire as they always did. Once again, Corrine sat next to the Chieftain on the ground, only now she was able to use Dante as a pillow as he laid next to his mother.

Arryn sat between her father and her aunt, Cathillian having gone to fetch a pitcher of wine.

"Alexander?" Corrine said. The Chieftain looked down at her with a smile on his face. "You never told us how you found Zobig. I'd like to hear about how you met him and bonded with him. Also, why he's such a grump."

Everyone began to laugh at her last comment, knowing it was true. Zobig truly was a big grump, but he was also a sweetheart. Arryn couldn't help but notice that he and Snow had been on much friendlier terms since the dark druid attack, and imagined it was because they had been forced to work together.

"Hmm," the Chieftain said, stroking the end of his long hair. "I believe I can do something like that. It really is quite an amusing story, and the reason why he's such a grump is because I just happened to stumble upon the grumpiest black bear in the entire forest."

The bear grumbled, thumping his back foot against the Chieftain's chair. The Chieftain saw it coming, both out of habit from his familiar, as well as through the bond.

Everyone laughed, and he adjusted his chair and cleared his throat.

CHAPTER SIXTEEN

After Alaric had left the Dark Forest for the crimes against their people, Alexander spent several days mourning his friend. He felt his loss on a deep level, even though he knew Alaric's absence was necessary for everyone's safety. His old friend had to go, but that didn't mean Alexander didn't feel regret, even if Alaric's actions were not his own.

To relax, he decided to go hunting. The meat had run out, and everyone had been so busy building that no one had gone for a hunt, and all they'd had to eat for a couple of days was fruit and vegetables.

That desperately needed to change. Alexander offered to do it himself, so he could take the time to be alone and not have to worry about prying eyes. Everyone seemed to worry so much for him, but he didn't want them to. He would be fine once he had processed everything.

Over time, his ability to speak to animals had gotten stronger, but he was still unable to bring larger animals to him—especially if they were very far away. Because of that, he still had to hunt the old-fashioned way: with a bow. But he didn't mind. It made him feel more connected to nature somehow.

Every step he made was incredibly light, as he was mindful of the twigs and dead leaves on the ground. If he did manage to find a target, he didn't want to scare it off. The woods had been home to many animals, but since the arrival of Alexander and his people, the forest had grown much thicker and animals had begun to move in from other less impacted parts of the forest.

After an hour or so, he had wandered quite a distance away from the barrier, but even further out, he saw exactly what he was after. Slowly, quietly, he crept closer to the large buck, kneeling as he pulled his bow from his shoulder, and nocked an arrow.

He took steady aim. When he loosed, though, the light wind affected his shot, causing him to hit the deer in the side of his neck.

The moment it struck, Alexander knew his mistake; he hadn't considered the wind, as his mind had been too cluttered to focus. He took an unclean shot, and now the deer was fleeing for its life.

Alexander jumped to his feet, running as quickly as he could manage. He had already made the initial mistake; he certainly didn't want to make another by causing the deer to suffer as it died—or worse, hit him in a non-vital area, and leave the deer be doomed to live with his injury.

It took several minutes to track the deer, and even longer to find him, but when he did, the buck was lying on the ground, breathing heavily. He looked weak, and guilt overrode Alexander's common sense. In a rush to end the deer's suffering, he approached too quickly.

Sensing danger, the deer jumped to his feet and kicked backward, his hooves smashing Alexander directly in the face. The Chieftain felt several bones crunch as he was thrown back into a tree, hit his head hard, and fell to the ground. Blood ran down his face, some of it getting into his eyes and burning them mercilessly.

He felt weak and dizzy, and he could hardly see anything, only adding to his fear and sense of urgency. He tried to move, but was unable. He was in a state between consciousness and unconsciousness. Just before his eyes fluttered closed, he saw the deer stumble and fall to the ground, and heard a loud roar echo through the immediate area.

Sometime later—he couldn't be sure just how long—his eyes began to lighten, and he was able to open them again. As he came around and started to remember what had happened, he was immediately greeted with the sound of loud sniffing. It sounded almost like a large dog, only a hundred times bigger.

Slowly, he cracked open his right eye. He saw a large black bear, straddling him, sniffing his face and chest and down to his stomach before making his way back up again, and it took everything he had not to jerk.

Instinct begged him to flop over onto his stomach, get his feet underneath him, and take off running as fast as possible. Logic, however, told him that he was injured, and even if he wasn't, there was no way he could outrun a bear.

A low grumble emanated from the bear, and Alexander looked up, both eyes open, to see the animal's eyes locked on his. As he saw the bear realize he was awake, fear seized him and removed all desire to move or even breathe.

For several long moments, the fact that he was a magic user completely slipped his mind. When he remembered, it still did no good. Trying to calm his magic only caused his throbbing head to throb even harder; his weakness was exacerbated at the small attempt.

The bear grumbled again as he lowered his face to Alexander's, his wet nose touching the Chieftain's cheek as he sniffed him.

The bear grumbled, and somehow Alexander was able to feel the bear's irritation. He wondered if the bear had been hunting that deer. If so, he could understand why the bear would be so angry with him. Despite this, he began to feel at ease, sensing the bear was more annoyed than angry.

After another grumble, and a movement that almost looked like an exasperated shake of his head, the bear backed away, walking toward the deer. Alexander closed his eyes and pursed his lips. He wanted so badly to yell at the bear to leave him his kill, especially given how badly he had been injured in acquiring it, but he had more sense than that.

Just before the bear grabbed hold of the deer's neck, he looked back at Alexander. He got the sensation the bear was gloating as he made off with his kill.

"I should've gone fishing at the river," Alexander groaned, lying back.

THE CHIEFTAIN TOOK a few drinks of his wine as Zobig grumbled next to him. He didn't seem to care much for being made to look like the bad guy, though he enjoyed being the grumpy old man in the animal kingdom.

Zoe had jumped at the chance to use her abilities to create a visual, allowing everyone to see the story as if they were really there. While the Chieftain had never thought much about mental magic, he enjoyed everyone seeing his stories even more than he enjoyed telling them.

"He took that deer to be a dick, didn't he?" Arryn asked. She turned her gaze from the Chieftain to the bear. "Zobig, don't lie. You did, didn't you?"

He grumbled as he rolled over on his back, wiggling side to side as he rolled around. It was quite cute, and Arryn could sense his amusement; that had been *exactly* why he had done it. She shook her head and laughed.

"That's just him. That's always been him," the Chieftain said as he reached out and scratched the bear's belly. "It was a few days before I saw him again. I'll never forget that day. The Arcadians had come to the Dark Forest."

ONCE AGAIN, it was time to go hunting, but Alexander had learned his lesson: never again would he go alone. He took several men and headed back out to the forest.

The area directly around the barrier was the most densely populated with wildlife, but it was mostly squirrels, birds, and other small rodents. The larger animals wandered all over, and the deer were still hard to find.

The druids had been out for quite some time when a loud, pain-filled roar filled the forest.

"What the hell was that?" one asked.

Alexander recognized the sound almost immediately. Fear washed over him as something flashed through his mind. His mind began to show images of a different part of the forest. There were men everywhere. He was looking back and forth, spears being thrust at him.

But when he blinked and shook his head, he was still standing with his men where he had been only moments before.

Andy, one of his men, grabbed hold of his arm and shook him. "Are you okay?"

The Chieftain didn't bother responding. He ran toward the sound when, yet another pain-filled roar filled the air. His fellow druids quickly followed him, their weapons drawn as soon as they saw men in the distance.

"Are those Arcadians?" Andy asked.

"Yeah! And they caught a bear!" Deni, a female warrior said.

"No one hurts the bear. I know him," Alexander ordered.

Andy and Deni both questioned him, but he didn't answer as he continued to run.

As soon as he was within reach, he threw out his right arm,

and a vine burst from the ground, wrapping around the arms of one of the guards thrusting a spear at the bear. Alexander moved his arm downward, and the guard's hands were violently pulled toward the ground, causing the guard to fall flat on his face.

The bear lunged forward, grabbed the guard's head in his large, powerful jaws, and clamped down. Alexander could hear the disgusting crunch even from where he stood.

The Arcadian guards rushed forward, attacking Alexander and his warriors. They were relatively matched in combat, but the warriors still trained longer every day, and did not have the arrogance that Adrien had instilled in his men. Arrogance made for easier targets.

One of them thrust a spear at Alexander, but he easily dodged it, kicking his leg up and over the long weapon to pin it at an angle. As expected, the Arcadian reached out for him. Alexander grabbed hold of the man's hand and yanked him closer, thrusting the knee that had previously held the spear into his opponent's ribs before punching him in the face and taking him down to the ground. With a quick twist of the neck, Alexander ended the man's life and moved on to the next.

After taking a punch to the face, his second opponent landed on the ground and threw his hands up, quickly backing away. "Please, let us go. We'll leave now and won't cause any more trouble."

Alexander heard three more men hit the ground, and he looked over to see his warriors ready to deal the final blows to their opponents. He turned back to face the man on the ground as gurgled screams echoed through the area.

"I'll let you live. Take your dead, put them in the cart that I know you have waiting not far from here for the resources you planned to steal from our land, and take them back to Adrien. Let him know I am *not* one to be messed with. I will not be tested. Please tell him if another Arcadian steps within the bounds of the Dark Forest, I will take it as a declaration of war. You just saw how easily we were able to take you down; don't think we couldn't do it again," he warned, his voice icy.

The man nodded wildly, his eyes wide as he quickly jumped up and grabbed the nearest fallen Arcadian, dragging the body back to the cart.

Alexander made his way over to the bear, moving slowly as he knelt next to the large steel trap he saw gripping the creature's leg. He pulled the metal jaws apart, seeing fresh blood and even bone as the bear pulled his leg free.

Without hesitation, Alexander reached out and pushed warmth through the bear, setting his bones and pulling the skin back together. The Chieftain stood and smiled at the bear as it regarded him with caution.

Once again, the bear grumbled. Then he bumped his massive shoulder into Alexander hard enough to knock him off balance. He landed hard on the ground, but something about the bear amused him, and he couldn't help but laugh.

"What a dick," Andy said, looking at the bear as he extended a hand to help Alexander up.

The Chieftain just smiled and shook his head. "I love that cranky bastard."

A FEW DAYS had passed since the Arcadians had tried to sneak into the Dark Forest to steal resources and had hunted on their land, and Alexander had not seen the bear. Logically, he felt relieved about that; without the ability to charm larger creatures, running into a bear was the last thing in the world he should want to do.

Still, deep down he couldn't help but feel a sense of loss. There was just something about that bear that he liked. He had a lot of personality, a lot of strength. He also had one hell of an attitude, and it made Alexander laugh. He wondered just what other personality quirks the large bear was hiding.

Alexander had just finished building a fire when screams erupted from a short distance away. His head shot up as he looked in the direction where they had come from, and heard another scream get cut off.

"Warriors!" Alexander shouted.

Men and women that he had trained alongside began tearing through the village, running as fast as they could to keep up with their Chieftain. More screams sounded, telling Alexander just how close they were. As his people approached the site, he saw two large lycanthropes, each chewing on one of his people.

Rage filled him as he ran forward. He couldn't tell if the women were alive or dead, but he wanted to save them if he could. Alexander ran for the savage on the left—a large, black beast with a silver chest and stomach—while the other charged his warriors.

The lycanthrope repeatedly swung his massive, clawed hands at Alexander's head. He ducked and rolled out of the way several times to avoid being struck. It would only take one hit to kill him if it landed right. These creatures were powerful, and he didn't plan on dying today.

He pulled a knife from his belt as he dove to the ground in a roll; then he got back up on his feet, turned, and threw it. The blade sank into the beast's rib cage, no doubt striking one of his lungs. He rumbled a deep, bone-chilling growl as he ripped the knife out and threw it back.

Alexander tried to dive out of the way, but it struck him in the leg, hitting his femoral artery. Though the creature had no skill in throwing knives, it had certainly been lucky. He pulled it free and attempted to heal himself before the lycanthrope attacked again, but he only had enough time to close the artery. He was still losing a lot of blood at a rapid pace, but the injury wouldn't be immediately fatal.

His movements much slower now, Alexander was unable to dodge the next attack. As the blow connected, the beast's hand rolled off his shoulder and struck him on the side of the head, throwing him several feet. He landed on the ground, his ears ringing, and the world around him spinning, and knew the only reason he was still alive was because his shoulder had taken the brunt of the impact.

Another scream sounded, and was immediately cut off as the second beast bit into the throat of one of his warriors. Alexander tried to roll over onto his stomach, but his larger, much more powerful opponent stepped on his side, rolling him over, before planting a foot on his chest to hold him down.

Alexander swallowed as fear radiated through him. Staring upward into the eyes of what he was certain was death itself, he tried to think of something, anything to do, but came up short. He was too weak, and had lost too much blood. The beast reached a massive clawed hand into the air, ready to strike the final blow, but a loud roar distracted him.

Alexander recognized it as the sound of an angry bear. He didn't have long to think about it before another horrifying growl ripped through the night sky. Everything seemed to stand still as he turned his head toward the barrier surrounding the Dark Forest.

It wasn't nearly as thick or strong as it would grow to be in the years to come, but it was still jagged and dangerous. His eyes widened as the barrier almost blew apart, and a large, black bear came busting through, the thorns and vines ripping and pulling at his skin and fur.

Within seconds, the bear was standing on its hind legs, dwarfing the lycanthrope in height and weight.

The bear swung a powerful front paw, connecting with the beast's jaw and knocking him off balance. The bear then dropped down on all fours and rushed his opponent, taking him down to the ground and sinking his teeth into the beast's throat before ripping him to shreds.

Alexander's eyes began to grow heavy as he lay there, bleeding profusely from his leg. He heard screams and yelling, and then he heard nothing. He tried to move, but he couldn't; all he could do was lie there and breathe. He could feel his body trying to heal, but without active magic, it would take a few minutes for him to regain even the slightest bit of energy.

He heard footsteps approaching, and the bear collapsed next to him. He was breathing hard, and his eyes were heavy. Alexander could smell the blood, and knew the bear had torn himself apart breaking through the barrier; though it was hard to determine just how many injuries he had sustained while fighting.

Alexander felt hands on his body, and then heat flowing through him as the energy began to grow. His fellow warriors were healing him, giving him life once again.

As soon as he was able to move, he rolled over to face the bear, placing his head against that of the massive animal lying next to him. "Thank you for your sacrifice," he said softly. "You risked your life to save mine and those of my people, but today is not your day to die." The Chieftain placed a weak hand on the side of the bear's face, sending his magic through.

Soon, the bear's breathing became even, and he began to stir.

"We are tied together, you and me. I can feel it. You are mine, and I am yours," the druid told him.

The bear just grumbled as he knocked Alexander over onto his back, and flopped his large head down on his chest.

EVERYONE WAS silent as the story of how the Chieftain and Zobig had bonded came to an end. They were all moved by how the bear had been prepared to sacrifice himself to save the Chieftain.

"When I had the vision of those men with the spears, and I was seeing through his eyes, I didn't understand it, but I knew something was happening between me and the bear. But when he saved me and came to lay down next to me, I could feel the relief flowing through him. Relief that he made it in time, that he had rescued me, and that was when I knew. There was no way he and I would ever be separated again."

Over the telling of the story, his familiar had lifted his head to lay on Alexander's lap. It wasn't often the druids saw Zobig be affectionate; understanding the Chieftain's story through their bond, and seeing it play out in Zoe's illusions had apparently had an effect on the creature, just as the telling of it had affected the Chieftain.

For once, everyone got to see the softer side of the grumpy old bear.

CHAPTER SEVENTEEN

Arryn pulled a sword from the weapons rack and inspected it. It was in terrible shape, but it would get the job done. They had decided to continue using the busted-up swords and other weapons for training purposes until the war was over. They didn't want to take a chance on ruining their new weapons before the battle even began.

Watching Roger work, Arryn had learned a few things about steel, and how it could be manipulated by magic. The problem was that solely using magic took a lot out of the magician, and very few weapons could be crafted at a time. Especially by someone who wasn't experienced.

Arryn wrapped her hand around the practice blade, knowing there was no sharp edge. Her eyes flashed black as she focused her power into her palm and fingers. Within seconds, the steel had begun to heat up and turn red. As it did, she slowly moved her hand down the length of steel, bending it back into shape.

As she got to the end—the sword was much straighter, though it still held a lot of nicks and dings—she pulled moisture from the air, wrapping it around her hand before freezing it. She then wrapped her hand around the sword, rapidly cooling it as she again moved her hand down the blade.

"Nice trick," her father said with a smile as he stepped into the pit.

She smiled as she flapped her hand around, trying to warm it without magic. "Yeah, well, the shitty thing is that it actually took more energy than larger things I've done. I've used a shit ton of magic before, and in comparison, this packed a punch."

He smiled. "Well, you're manipulating steel. The magic required to manipulate or transmogrify items is far more exhausting than regular magic."

She nodded. "Good to know. So, you ready to get your butt kicked?"

Laughing, he shook his head. "Are you sure about that? It's been a while, but I feel pretty confident I can still wield a sword. What about you? You're using a practice sword, and mine is real. What if I cut you, or worse?"

Arryn snorted. "Cathillian has stabbed me in the gut before; I have run him through a time or two, also. It'll be fine, I promise."

He stared at her with a shocked expression. "That's normal around here?"

She shrugged, nodding. "Trust me, there's no better instructor than pain. We only train that hard in the advanced warrior training. For those just wanting to learn self-defense, it's not that dangerous."

"What about Corrine? She's going into the warrior training. She's even starting early, from what I've gathered."

She sighed. "Corrine is an exception. Normally, the Chieftain would never allow one so young to take part in the violent training, but she's not a normal kid. She's been on her own since she was old enough to walk, and she's taken care of herself this entire time. Because of her experiences, she's aged far more in her short eight years then many adults I know. That's why the Chieftain gave his blessing, and why, when he asked me, I gave my blessing, too. If she doesn't like it, she doesn't have stick with it—but I've seen her determination. That little girl is going to be a force to be reckoned with."

Christopher smiled. "Well, if she's anything like her adoptive mother, then I would have to say you're right on that. She looks up to you. She idolizes you. I can't say that's a bad thing. You enrich the lives of everyone around you, especially mine. And I don't want to look bad in front of my daughter, so I'm excited to see just what I can do with you as my sparring partner."

Arryn was moved by her father's words. At her age, it was hard to think of herself as an adoptive mom to Corrine, though she knew that was how the girl saw her. Not as her best friend, not as her big sister, but as her mom.

Though Arryn had no idea how to be a mom, she wanted to do the best she possibly could for the girl—no matter the role Corrine had chosen her to play. She would be whatever she needed to be for her.

"Corrine is going to get her ass kicked in training, and hard. If she decides to stick with it, she will have more bad days than good in the beginning. But as she grows older, no one will be able to stop her. Just like you. You're about to get your ass kicked, and hard, but I'll teach you a few lessons." Arryn winked and smiled, and her father smiled back.

"Let the match begin," he said.

Without warning, Arryn immediately lunged forward. She thrust the sword out in front of her, and Christopher easily jumped to the side. As he did, he spun, swinging his sword around and aiming for her side. Arryn dropped to her knees, leaning back to allow his blade to go over her head. She came back up, and he was still open from his move. She thrust her sword into his stomach.

The blunted end hit him hard, causing him to grunt as he doubled over. Had he been any other opponent, she would have jumped to her feet and thrust her knee into his face—but she knew he had suffered at the hands of Aeris, and she couldn't bring herself to do it.

"Are you okay?" she asked.

Her father took a deep breath, steeling himself as he straightened. "Are you going to ask me that every time you make contact?"

She shrugged. "Had you been anyone else, you would've gotten a knee to the face. I'm trying to ease you into this."

He smiled and shook his head. "A lot has changed in the short time you were gone. Elysia and the mystic have helped me a lot. Don't pull your punches; I kind of like the idea of how you guys train. Besides, I used to be the best in the city with a sword— clearly, I'm a little rusty, but I'll catch up quickly, don't you worry."

She nodded. "Very well then. As of right now, you're not my father; you are my opponent, and I am yours. Don't pull punches with me, either, I assure you I can take anything you dish out."

Christopher took a deep breath, exhaling shakily before nodding. "Again."

Arryn once more rushed forward, raising her sword. At the last second, she dropped to her knees, spun around, and thrust the handle of her sword into the back of his knee, causing him to lose his balance.

As he fell to the ground, she twisted enough to throw an elbow into his face. Nothing broke, but she could hear bone grinding against bone as she made impact. Without hesitation, she lowered her blade to his neck.

"Point to me," Arryn said.

To her surprise, Christopher laughed as he reached for his nose. "That hurt like hell, but I don't think it's broken."

Arryn shook her head. "If I'm honest, that wasn't on purpose. I was at a bad angle, so I couldn't get the power behind it that I wanted. Definitely bad form, but if I had been back just a couple more inches, I probably would have broken it."

He laughed, then groaned as he rolled to sit up. "Good to know you didn't take it easy on your old man."

Smiling, she clapped him on the back. "I'm just an obedient child." She stood, extending her hand. "Ready to get your ass kicked again?"

He looked at her with admiration. Reaching out his hand and accepting hers, he said, "Absolutely."

———

IT WAS A BEAUTIFUL DAY; the sun was shining down through the canopy of the trees. But as Arryn sat in her favorite spot by the river, the clear skies now in full view, she couldn't help but worry about what was to come.

The truth was that no one had any idea what was coming, or when. Arryn had killed several dark druids on her way out of their encampment, including two of their most powerful, Aeris and Jenna. Jenna hadn't been a dark druid for long, she seemed to be a prodigy in the dark arts. She certainly never had any talent for pure nature magic.

So, what exactly was to come?

The dark druids weren't the type to give up or back down, and Arryn had no reason to believe they would do so now. No one in the villages believed that, either. But what exactly could they do? Their numbers had dwindled with every attack, and there was no way they could hope to take the Dark Forest with the warriors they currently had.

That only allowed them the option of recruitment, and, desperate or not, Arryn couldn't see them scouring the farmlands and knocking on doors to ask for help. Outside of Arcadia, people were still terrified of druids, dark or otherwise.

So, were they preparing for nothing? Were they worried of an impending attack at any given moment for nothing?

The elders had discussed the timeline, what they might

expect, and their proposal was to be proactive. The druids of the Dark Forest never went looking for a fight, but they sure as hell wouldn't turn away from one if it found them.

Things were about to change.

The Chieftain had decided that very morning that if the final war did not begin soon, he would set out and hunt down Alaric himself. He would take an army with him, of course, but one way or another, this fight *would* end.

The druids had had enough.

As for Arryn, she had made a promise, and she fully intended to keep it. It didn't matter to her if she was the one to deliver the final blow to Alaric and Jerick; deep down, she actually hoped it would be the Chieftain. But either way, her promise would be kept.

She rather liked threatening those who would bring harm to others; making them relive her words in their minds over and over again, until she made good on them.

She sat next to the water, in the lotus position: her hands lying on her knees with her palms facing up. She inhaled deeply through her nose and exhaled through her mouth as her eyes closed. Meditation was relatively new for her, but she rather liked it. It allowed her to focus and get in touch with her magic much faster.

And the energy boost when weakened certainly didn't hurt.

Her eyes flashed both black and green as she used her physical magic, pushing it down into the earth to allow her connection. She felt down through the ground. Without digging, she knew the location of every rock, every piece of glass long buried, and every other hardened material.

With her nature magic, she connected to the wind and to the water in front of her, allowing the scents of nature to wrap around her as she focused on the elements.

As she sat, her heightened level of awareness clued her in to someone approaching. She reached out with her nature magic and sensed a familiar life force.

Cathillian.

"I can sense you a mile away," he told her as he passed over the forest threshold, onto the beach of the river. "You shine like a star with the magic you're using. What are you doing here?"

She held her position. "I'm doing an experiment." She briefly looked over at him before giving him a wink and a smile. "Don't you worry. You'll see soon enough."

She closed her eyes again and felt him sit next to her. She knew he wasn't going away anytime soon; not that she minded, but she planned on giving him a hard time about it anyway if she had the chance.

"What are you doing out here?" she asked.

"The twins talked to the Chieftain this morning, shortly after you left. I felt you should be aware of the game plan."

She looked at him with genuine curiosity. "What's happening?"

He picked up a rock and played with it, turning it over and over in his fingers. "Bast and Cleo requested to be on the front line when the time comes. If we are attacked at random, there's no way to prepare for that, but they know we plan to initiate if the dark druids don't. If that happens, they want to be up front."

Arryn didn't even hesitate. "No. Absolutely not," she shook her head. "They have offered their services, and as far as I'm concerned, we are indebted to them. The arrangement was once they helped us, we would go help them. But this goes above and beyond. I won't allow them to stand at the front and take the first impact when this isn't their fight."

Cathillian laughed. "You've come a long way. You surprise me every day; you surprise all of us every day. Somehow, you have managed to move from being an Arcadian, to the Arcadian druid, then to Arcadian druid warrior."

Arryn moved into a more comfortable position, leaning back

on her hands as she focused on the water. "And what have I evolved into now?"

She could see him smile at her out of her peripheral. "Somehow, you've catapulted your way to the top, taking on responsibility and exhibiting incredible strength in battle tactics and execution. You have taken on the role of an elder. Alongside my mother, I feel like both of you are generals of our army."

She smiled. "Why do I feel like there's a 'but' coming?"

"Well, I felt like I should butter you up and tell you how epic you are before saying that you have no right to say 'no' to the twins. They are not *your* responsibility. They are warriors, which means they are responsible for themselves. On top of that, you have to remember that the Chieftain has the five stars—he calls the shots. He's let you lead us, and you haven't let us down even once. But he has agreed to let them do this, and I am behind him all the way."

She flashed him in icy look. "You think it's okay to shove our guests to the front line and hide behind them like cowards? Also, five stars? What?"

He waved a hand. "It was something I learned about from the Arcadian Guard trainees. They knew how militaries used to be run." He shook his head. "That's beside the point. Did you not hear the things that Amelia said about the twins? We haven't seen them fight because every one of us, including you, is too scared to get in the pit with them; not one of us wants to take a punch from them. If they want to go out in front, there's probably a damn good reason why. Don't you want to see what they're capable of? Don't you want to know who we have agreed to go to war with when all this is over?"

She sighed, shaking her head as she looked out at the water.

He continued. "When we leave the forest, we are at their mercy. We literally have no idea where we're going. We have no idea what we're going to see, what we're going to be up against. If those girls are behind us when we go into battle with the dark druids, how the hell will we know if they survived on their own merit, or by someone else repeatedly saving their ass?

"I don't know about you, but if they're badass enough to believe they belong in front with us, I think we should give it to them. Let's use this as an opportunity to see exactly what they're capable of. Because when we leave the Valley, I want to make sure that your life is not being put in the hands of two people who don't care about protecting it. I won't do it. I would hope that you felt the same for me."

She sighed again, thinking over his words. She didn't want to admit it, but his reasoning made perfect sense. Amelia said the girls were capable of throwing punches hard enough to make their insides look like they had jumped off a tall building.

If that was true, along with their ability to move a ton of earth at one time without breaking a sweat, they could probably slow down an approaching army.

Finally, she nodded. "If they want to be up front, we'll let them. Let's see what they can do. As for you..." She turned toward him again, a warm smile on her face. "You need to stop worrying about me so much."

He smiled as he reached over and grabbed her, pulling her around to sit in his lap. "I always worry about you. I can't help it. It's been that way since we were little, and it will be that way until the day I die."

Arryn leaned forward and kissed him, which he happily reciprocated. She had been so stressed out, worrying about what was to come and how it might happen, that she hadn't allowed herself time to relax and enjoy the people around her, the life around her.

She decided that was going to change.

She lunged forward, knocking him down to the ground before kissing him again. There was no time like the present to experience everything life had to offer.

CHAPTER EIGHTEEN

It was late in the evening when Nika called everyone to the pit. Corrine stood off to the side, tapping her foot anxiously as she tried to calm herself.

She had been training nonstop, and Nika believed she was ready to give a demonstration. Corrine wasn't quite as sure, but she didn't want to let her instructor down when she believed in her so much.

Bast and Cleo had both taken an interest in her, and taught her even more about throwing punches. They had gotten along swimmingly, and Corrine had become quite close to them in a short time.

"If you win, I'll braid your hair like I do Cleo's," Bast offered.

Corrine's eyes widened as a smile broke out on her face, and she nodded. "I'd love that!" she admitted excitedly.

She struggled every day to keep her long, kinky, textured hair out of her face while training. It was difficult for her to control, mostly because she had never much cared.

No one had taught her how to care for her hair—or for herself, for that matter. It wasn't until she came to the Dark

Forest that she learned about proper hygiene and how to even tie her hair back. She and Arryn were both still learning how to control her locks.

Bast and Cleo both had textured hair like Corrine's. Bast kept hers straight, using physical magic and her fingers to iron it out with heat pulsing through her skin, while her sister liked hers in tight box braids. Corrine liked the idea of her hair being braided like Cleo's.

The twins each wished her luck before walking way. She smiled as more familiar faces wandered up.

"Not gettin' nervous, are ye?" Samuel asked. "There might be five years between you and yer opponent, but ye have heart, lass. Don't let 'er get the best of ye."

Corrine nodded, taking a deep breath and exhaling slowly as she tried to steel herself. Samuel and Celine each gave her a hug before leaving to find their placement in the ever-growing crowd.

Looking around, Corrine saw the Chieftain standing at the head of the pit, with Elysia, Cathillian, Arryn, the twins, and now Samuel and Celine close by.

They're all here, she thought to herself.

"Thanks for coming, everyone," Nika said with a radiant smile. "Ryel and I have been working to train our students as well as our teenage recruits, and, as always, we couldn't be prouder of our young warriors. But sometimes, we have a student that sticks out above the rest. Around here, that's something to celebrate—not be jealous of."

Corrine felt a blush come to her cheeks. She saw Arryn smiling at her with pride and love, and Cathillian and the others wearing similar expressions.

Just breathe, and don't let them down.

"We called all of you here because we have such a student. As all of you know, Corrine came from a place where differences weren't celebrated; they were feared. Since coming here, she has gone from not understanding our ways and even being afraid of taking even the tiniest punch, to demanding to be accepted into full warrior training.

"I'm sure you can imagine our shock, given that she is only eight years old. We have never had someone that young want to take the training, because it's rigorous and violent. But as a community, we listen to our children and to one another. Instead of deciding for someone else what they are capable of, we allow them to take a step forward and try.

"We didn't pick her opponent; the opponent picked herself. Her peers are so proud of her that they each took to the pit, sparring against one another for the right to fight Corrine here today."

Corrine's eyes widened. She hadn't been aware of that. She looked over to her friend, Emily, to see her smile and give a curt nod. To know she had literally fought her way to the top to help Corrine show off and celebrate her newly acquired skills almost brought tears to her eyes.

Ryel turned to Corrine. "Win or lose, Corrine, this is a success. This match isn't to prove you're better, but to show off just how great you are, and how much you have learned." He stepped back and gestured for her to enter farther into the pit.

She nodded and approached her opponent, giving a salute as she had been taught.

"Good luck," Emily said with a smile as she stepped back to her own side.

Once again, Corrine took a deep breath. She shook her hands, trying to dry the thin sheen of sweat that coated her palms.

"Begin!" Nika shouted.

Corrine immediately took a defensive position, putting her fists up as she studied her opponent. She watched Emily in hopes of catching some kind of a sign. When she saw nothing aside from the young woman also taking her own defensive position, Corrine decided to make the first move.

She charged her opponent, leaping forward and landing on her hands as she tumbled just to Emily's side. She quickly rolled her feet, jumping up and landing on the girl's back, quickly taking her down to the ground. Emily landed hard, and Corrine quickly pinned her arms down.

"Point to Corrine!" Nika shouted.

Corrine rolled off and helped Emily to her feet. The older girl nodded at Corrine, a warrior's sign of respect.

The girls waited for several moments before Nika announced the start of the round.

Emily began this time, but Corrine didn't hesitate. Running forward, Corrine sidestepped a kick that was aimed for her stomach before ducking under a punch. When Emily recoiled, Corrine lashed out, punching the girl in the ribs. Emily recovered quickly, as Corrine's angle hadn't been right, and she hadn't used enough power to throw her off.

As Corrine prepared to punch Emily again, Emily's fist moved like lightning, shooting forward and striking her right in the face. Corrine felt the bone above her brow crunch, the punch sliding downward into her nose as well. In one hit, Emily had successfully broken her brow bone and the bridge of her nose.

Corrine stumbled backwards, but she didn't fall. Instead, she felt white-hot rage as the pain radiated through her head.

Letting out a battle cry, Corrine ran forward. Once she was within reach, she came to a dead halt, bent over, folding herself in half, and then whipped her leg upward, smashing the girl in the face with her heel. As Emily stumbled back, Corrine righted herself and rushed forward to punch her in the stomach, before pulling back and slamming an elbow across her face.

Emily dropped to her knees, and Corrine quickly ran behind her. She knelt down and wrapped her arm around Emily's throat, putting her in a hold that would allow Corrine to break her neck.

"Point to Corrine!" Nika shouted.

In a real match, Corrine's move would have been a deathblow. She had won.

Shouts and cheers erupted as Corrine let her opponent go. She stood and extended her hand, which Emily happily took. Corrine's emerald eyes flashed bright, neon green as she pushed magic from her hand into Emily's, healing her wounds.

"Sorry about that," Corrine said.

Emily grunted as her nose set in place, twitching it several times before sniffling a bit. She dropped her hand and smiled at Corrine. "Don't be sorry. You won fair and square. I didn't go easy on you, but I'm glad you overpowered me. This day was for you."

Arryn, Cathillian, and the elders made their way over with smiles on their faces.

"You did awesome!" Arryn said, reaching up and laying her hand on the side of Corrine's face.

Corrine had taken the time to heal Emily, but not herself. Heat flooded through her cheek and to the rest of her face as Arryn's magic washed over her. She closed her eyes and grunted as she felt her nose snap back into place and her brow bone lift and stitch itself back together. Within moments, the pain was gone, and she opened her eyes to see Arryn smiling at her still.

Every day it felt like she learned all over again what it was like to be loved and be part of the family. She couldn't believe just how supportive of her they were and how much they believed in her.

"I knew you could do it," Arryn said. "I'm so proud of you. Before you know it, you'll be kicking everybody's ass and taking names."

Corrine smiled. "Does this mean I can go with you when you go to Kemet?"

Arryn looked over to Bast and Cleo; both had guilty looks on their faces. She turned back to face Corrine. "Is that why you're doing all this?"

Corrine shrugged. "Not the only reason. I know you'll be leaving soon, and it's not like I'll be alone or anything, but I still don't want to be without you. I love it here, and I love everyone, but I don't want to say goodbye to you. I thought if I was strong enough, you might take me along."

She hadn't actually spoken the words out loud before, but knowing Arryn would be leaving soon had played a big part in her decision to do more training. Her fear of not being able to help the one she loved had been the biggest catalyst throughout.

Arryn sighed as she took Corrine's hands in hers. "This is a big decision, and one I'm not sure I'm ready to make. I feel like taking you with me would be very irresponsible of me. I don't want to take you with me and risk your life, but I also don't want to leave you behind. I know I'm not your birth mom, but I don't want you to feel like I'm abandoning you or don't want to be around you."

Corrine looked down to the ground, nodding. Arryn's answer had been disappointing, but she hoped she would change her mind.

Arryn smiled as she placed a finger under Corrine's chin to lift her gaze. "How about I promise that we'll talk about this after the battle? I think once everything is over, we will be able to think more clearly. I'm not saying yes, but I'm not saying no, either. And I think this should be a decision that we all make as a family. Not just you and I—all of us."

Corrine looked at her with curiosity. "Like a vote?"

Nodding, Arryn said, "Yeah. Like a vote. That way, we hear everyone's thoughts, and we take into consideration what everyone has to say. Then we can make an informed decision."

Corrine thought for a few moments and then smiled. "I can live with that."

Arryn pulled her into a hug, and Bast made her way over. "You kicked her ass. You ready to get your box braids?"

Her entire face lit up as she stepped away from Arryn and nodded with excitement. "Yes!"

She waved to Arryn and the others before leaving with Bast, holding hands with her and Cleo.

CHAPTER NINETEEN

In all his years, Alaric had never once used a magitech weapon, and it was something he never thought he would consider, but there they were. Desperate times called for desperate measures, and he couldn't deny the possibilities that existed with using magitech in this fight.

For a week, Locke's men trained the dark druids how to aim and how to shoot. They had been terrible at first, but most picked it up surprisingly fast. He couldn't help but think Aeris would have been great at it; then Alaric remembered his diehard affinity for laws, and knew he never would have agreed.

Good riddance.

The past few days, they had trained as they moved. Alaric, Jerick, and their dark druids, along with Locke and his hundred men, all moved toward the Dark Forest. Alaric had no way of knowing how this would go, but with his brother, he truly believed victory was inevitable.

Jerick had been working hard to create an antidote for the smoke, one that would allow them to touch it and breathe it without problems. While they didn't have enough time to come up with anything completely effective, he was able to craft a lotion that would protect the skin, and an herbal oil that could be either ingested or smoked to protect the throat and the alveoli in the lungs.

Some damage would still occur, but a little irritation and coughing was certainly better than ruptured blood vessels in the lungs, filling up their chest cavities, causing them to drown in their own fluids.

Everyone had already begun using the lotion, wanting to be prepared for anything. It wouldn't take much for them to ingest or smoke the oil if they sensed enemies approaching, but taking the time to apply the lotion would be impossible.

"What if they're waiting for us?" one of the dark druids asked.

Alaric rolled his eyes, annoyed. He almost felt like even asking that showed doubt in his plan, his abilities. "Then we will have them on our turf, now won't we? Their strength lies in the plants. Like a physical magic user, it takes more energy for them to create something out of nothing than it does to use what's already there. In our neck of the woods, everything is dead. They can't use anything."

"*Oooh*," the dark druid said, nodding his head.

Alaric sighed as he increased his speed. Jerick looked over at him and smiled. "Trouble with the commoners?"

Alaric almost laughed. While his people weren't very smart, they were loyal. "Always. Can't handle stupidity, especially right now. I need every ounce of brainpower I have to focus on what's ahead, especially if I have to think for all of these imbeciles as well."

"I feel your pain on that," Locke said. "Unfortunately, you either have to get used to it, or empower them. Once you start educating them, and they learn a few things, they start thinking they're better than everyone else. That's when you have to establish dominance and pop a couple of eyes out of their sockets. Fuck all that. I think it's better to have them stupid and loyal, than smart but arrogant enough to challenge you."

Alaric did laugh then. "I suppose I hadn't really thought of it in those terms. In that case, I'd have to say you're right about that."

"Okay, so here's the plan," Jerick said. "When we reach the southern edge of the Dark Forest, we will drop our large bags in the cave and take only the supplies we need. Food won't be a problem, because we can hunt and there's plenty of vegetation on their side; we can take our fill before they even sense us."

The sound of loud growling caught their attention. All three leaders were immediately on high alert, looking around. Alaric and Jerick quickly identified the culprit. Two wolves were fighting ahead, males trying to determine the alpha among their pack.

One of the wolves, the slightly larger one, grabbed the other by the neck, and throwing him into a tree only a couple of feet away. Several birds in the tree took flight. Alaric thought the birds would probably linger, not wanting to leave their nests while wolves were fighting underneath, and he was proven right as the birds swarmed overhead.

Shaking his head, he gestured to his brother. "They're just having a squabble over dominance, go on."

"Anyway, if all goes well, we should arrive back to the cave in twelve or so hours. Depending on how fast we travel and how little we sleep, we could be resting in our new home in the Dark Forest in another thirty-six to forty-eight hours," Jerick finished.

***

SINCE IT HAD BEEN DECIDED that if the war didn't come to them in a short time, they would seek it out, the druids of the Dark Forest had begun taking extreme measures. Everyone was on high alert, rushing around to prepare for the worst. Arryn had just made her way back into the main village after overseeing the project she had asked the twins to undertake, when she saw the Chieftain kneeling by two wolves.

"What's going on?" Arryn asked, having recognized the wolves as scouts.

The Chieftain stood and smiled. "We have news." He gave each of the wolves a scratch under the chin before coming to stand next to her. "I sent the two largest males South, along with a flock of birds. I instructed them to fight one another. If they were simply lurking around, I knew Alaric would be suspicious."

Arryn smiled. "Fight for alpha?"

He nodded, also smiling. "They did a pretty good job, too; they got rowdy and 'disturbed' a flock of birds, and the birds were then able to get close. The dark druids were close to home when the wolves and birds found them. Once they get back to the cave, they'll be making quick preparations and heading this way. That means we have somewhere around forty-eight hours, give or take, based on the time it took the wolves to return."

"Good. We'll be ready for them. I wasn't about to take the risk of them using the smoke again, so I took some initiative myself."

"Oh? What did you do?" the Chieftain asked.

Cathillian and Elysia both walked over, and she saw Celine, Samuel, and her father approaching from another direction. She waited for them to arrive, then began to speak.

"Because of how the dark druids attacked the last time, I took the twins with me to the river, well outside of the barrier, and we used magic to create a ditch that loops around. We then allowed the river to fill it, providing us with an endless supply of water. If they begin to blow smoke into the area, we can use the water to absorb and disperse it, as well as put out the flames causing it," Arryn said.

"Not to mention the endless ammo we'll have by creating ice shards," Celine said with a smile.

Arryn nodded. "Exactly; having constant access to the river

gives us endless possibilities. Mostly, my concern was for the smoke."

"Where are the twins now?" Elysia asked. "That much work would have been exhausting, even for them."

"I sent them to one of the guest cabins, so they could rest," Arryn replied.

The Chieftain nodded. "You are one of our most powerful assets, so we need you rested, as well. We have no idea what's going to happen. Right now, I want you to go back to your own cabin and get some rest. Real rest. Sleep. This is *not* a discussion. We need you at your very best." He turned toward Cathillian. "I need you to send Echo south, and see if she can find the dark druids. We need to know how far out they are, and how much time we have, and she's the fastest we have."

Cathillian nodded then gave Arryn a soft smile before turning and walking away. She returned the smile, and as the Chieftain continued to give orders, Elysia eyed Arryn with obvious and extreme suspicion. A knowing, almost sly smile curved one corner of her mouth.

Arryn gave a curt nod and walked away. As she made her way toward her cabin, she increased her speed. Once she felt she was safely out of earshot, she began to run, knowing Elysia would ask questions. She didn't want to answer them. Not yet.

Unfortunately for her, Elysia was quite crafty.

Just as Arryn reached her cabin, Elysia dropped from the sky directly in front of her. A vine unwrapped from her waist and extended arm, as she gave Arryn the same smile she had several moments before.

"Arryn, so good to see you. I feel like we need to catch up," Elysia said with a strange tone to her voice.

"Well, the Chieftain said I needed to get some sleep, and I have to agree." She stretched her arms out and yawned, exaggerating the movements.

"Oh, I know, you definitely need to get some rest. We need you at your very best! Just like my father said."

An awkward silence hung in the air as Elysia stared her down. Arryn was for the first time in her entire life at a loss for words because she felt guilty. She had no reason to feel guilty, however, because; the druids had a much different mindset than the Arcadians did.

Love, relationships, and especially sex, were all considered completely natural. They didn't get hung up on marriage or a joined future; the only thing that mattered was that both parties were consenting and cared for one another, and that no one was getting hurt in the process.

But the Arcadian in her screamed, "*Guilty, guilty, guilty!*"

Elysia placed all of her weight on one foot, crossing the other over at the ankle, and crossed her arms over her chest. She quirked an eyebrow, and Arryn knew she knew.

The moment Elysia had looked at her as Cathillian walked away, Arryn knew Elysia knew; but Elysia wanted her honesty.

"Okay!" Arryn said loudly. "We did it. Out by the river. There, I said it. Are you happy now?"

The older woman smiled, taking a much more relaxed position before reaching out and pulling Arryn into a hug. "I always hoped the two of you would see past the silliness and senses of humor to see what the rest of us did."

Arryn suddenly felt overwhelmed with emotion.

"I always had a feeling you wanted the two of us to be together. Out of curiosity, what was it that you saw?" Arryn asked.

Elysia pulled back and smiled. "I saw my son find a best friend in you. Then over the years, it evolved. You turned into someone that he would die for, someone he would protect until his very last breath. That doesn't mean anything necessarily, other than my son had picked the person he wanted to be with. What made me, and everyone else, so hopeful was that we saw the exact same thing in you. You would be willing to die for him, to protect him no matter what the cost to yourself. We always knew, but you both have proven this time and time again. I'm glad you both finally accepted it."

Arryn could feel the color rising to her cheeks. It wasn't that she was uncomfortable talking about feelings—she was just uncomfortable talking about her own. She tried to look at it as a strength, not a weakness, but it was still difficult.

"You do realize I'm still going to punch him when he's being an ass, right?"

Elysia's head fell back and she laughed loudly. "And I'm sure that he will still pick on you and knock you out of your seat when you're being one. If I thought for an instant all that silliness would disappear, then the two of you wouldn't really belong together. Both of you seem to have the ability to put relationships aside for your duty to the tribe, and that's important. His father and I were much the same. Anyway, you need to get some sleep. I just remember the last conversation we had about this, and since you hadn't come to me directly, I figured I would help you with that." She gave a wink.

Arryn rolled her eyes. "Oh, thank you. I do *so* appreciate that."

Elysia gave her one last hug and kissed her on the cheek. She walked away without saying anything else.

Taking a deep breath and blowing it out with force, Arryn walked into her cabin, prepared to do her best to force herself to sleep.

CHAPTER TWENTY

Once the dark druids had reached their cave, Alaric and Jerick meticulously watched over their people as they gathered their things and made preparations. They couldn't afford for anything to go wrong, and wouldn't risk it.

As soon as that had been done, they were moving again.

It had been almost twenty-four hours, and they were already just over the halfway mark. Everyone now had magitech rifles in hand, while Locke's men carried various additional forms of magitech weapons—including a new magitech grenade Locke swore would tear a hole in the side of a mountain.

On the outside was a pressure switch that engaged a gear on the inside. That gear would tick several times before striking and smashing a small amphorald crystal, which would explode, sending tiny steel beads in different directions. The strength of the explosion would propel the steel balls fast and hard enough to cut through almost anything.

While Alaric didn't like the sound of tearing up his new home, he certainly didn't mind causing a few casualties to claim it.

Overhead, Alaric saw the largest golden eagle he'd ever seen circling. He had seen that bird before; it was hard to miss, and harder to forget.

"That's a familiar," Alaric said. "Alexander will soon know we're coming."

"So much for the element of surprise," Locke quipped.

"Are you able to reach it with your death touch?" Jerick asked.

Alaric shook his head. "Has to be within twenty to thirty feet. That bird knows to stay out of my way… Clearly, they've warned it about me."

"With the element of surprise off the table, we need to hurry and get ready," Jerick said.

Alaric stopped and turned to the crowd of druids and mercenaries behind him. "We need to move faster. From here on out, no sleep. That eagle that just flew above us will be our downfall. Before the sun reaches its apex tomorrow, we will be at war."

As soon as the sun rose, Arryn and the others began making their way toward the ditch that she and the twins had dug the day before. The water was flowing through nicely; she was happy to see it working so well.

As the Chieftain had instructed her to do, she had spent the rest of the entire previous day locked in her cabin. When she couldn't fall sleep, she had asked Zoe to knock her out.

It was the only thing that seemed to work.

The sun was much higher now, and everyone stood ready for whatever might happen. Echo had returned, and they knew it would be soon; Alaric had recognized her.

The druids were comfortable where they were, and knew Alaric and Jerick would attack head-on. It would be a mistake on their part, but Alexander had no doubt in his mind that Alaric would be arrogant enough to believe the army he had hired would be enough to take them down.

It was his old friend's worst characteristic—aside from the whole being-an-evil-dick part.

Arryn, Celine, and even Christopher stood at the edge of the river offshoot, ready to end it all. Up in the trees, the *Schatten* were hiding in absolute silence. All around them, animals stilled. Every man, woman, child, and creature in the forest could sense exactly what was at stake.

The birds did not chirp, and the squirrels stood and watched in the same direction the druids did. Several feet behind her, Snow lay on the ground; to her left was Zobig, and to her right was her son, Dante, who was now the size of a full-grown tiger despite his young age. This time, he would be able to fight along-side them, though he had strict instructions to stay close to his mother.

The other familiars were fanned out, and other animals had joined into the party.

Off in the distance, they heard the screams of animals.

Arryn looked over her shoulder. "What is that? What's happening?"

The Chieftain's fists clenched as his eyes narrowed, and he looked down to meet Arryn's gaze. His face was pure rage. "They're forcing the animals into submission. They're broadening their army." His eyes slowly lifted as they focused on the sounds in the distance.

Arryn turned, just as angry as he was. She remembered how the deer had screamed and become enraged when Corrine had tried to force it into submission. It hadn't gone well, but she was much younger than them, far less powerful. Between Jerick's druids, who were closer to natural druid magic, and Alaric, whose people used only dark nature magic, she had no doubt those animals would submit soon enough.

Flocks of birds took to the sky, flying overhead in frantic circles. They dove and shot back up, warning them.

"Arryn," the Chieftain said, his voice hard. "Ready yourselves. They've lit the fires."

Arryn nodded once, turning to look at Celine on her left and then her father on her right.

"Are you sure you're ready for this?" she asked him.

Her father smirked, a look she had never seen him use. It was dark and vengeful, and she liked it. "You bet your ass, I am. I'm going to make them suffer for keeping me away from you all these years."

Arryn smiled. "That's my dad. Just focus on all the pain they caused you. Trust me, that'll be enough to light that magic of yours right on fire. Speaking of which, hands out."

Arryn leaned forward first, placing her hands just inside the tiny creek bed they had created. Celine and Christopher followed suit. Each of them were still, the birds above now resting in the canopy overhead after having given their warning.

A loud screech sounded off overhead as Echo flew over, circling around and landing on the low branch of the tree nearest them.

"The smoke is approaching," Cathillian reported.

Arryn's eyes flashed black as she pushed her magic toward her hands, sending intense heat flowing through them. She felt the energy to her left and right; Celine and Christopher were doing the same. Steam began to roll off the water, just as the poisonous smoke began to blow into a visible area. Behind them, Arryn felt Cathillian, Elysia, and the Chieftain began to call wind.

They gently blew the steam forward. As it connected with the smoke, it mixed in, absorbing it into the steam's cloud. The idea was that once the smoke had mixed with it, the steam would fall to the ground as water, harming no one in the process.

"*Schatten!*" the Chieftain shouted out.

Arryn could hear only the faintest rustling of leaves as the *Schatten* rapidly moved through the canopy of thick trees. Each was armed with large canteens of water. They were to follow the steam, making sure to stay out of the reach of the smoke while continuing to push the steam back as far as it could reach. Once they arrived over the fires, they would put them out as quickly as possible, and kill the men lighting them.

Arryn wasn't exactly sure how well that part would go, but the shadow warriors were the best for that job because of their stealth—not even the dark druids would be able to sense them coming.

Within moments, birds began to flock overhead again. "They're walking through the smoke," Elysia said. "They must've found a way to make themselves invulnerable. They're trying to use smoke cover."

Echo called out again, and Cathillian gave an exuberant, "Fucking *yes*! Thank you, Echo," he said. "The *Schatten* were successful, but we did lose one. The fires are out. We should be clear from the smoke, now."

Arryn, her father, and Celine all dropped their magic, and the steam immediately turned back into its original water form, dropping to the ground. The forest would be able to absorb the poisons without any negative effects, as they had discovered with the earlier attack; the animals had only been mildly affected while the vegetation hadn't been affected at all.

"If what I'm seeing in the images from our messenger birds is correct, the dark druids have weapons. Magitech weapons," the Chieftain said.

Arryn stood, turning to look back at him. "They're using magitech?"

He nodded. "According to the wolves and scout birds we used, they came from south of the Heights. Didn't you say that that was where the bandits were originating from?"

Cathillian laughed. "Damn. We might get to end that little battle right here and now. We planned to go after them anyway. How nice of them to come to us instead."

Bast and Cleo stepped out from behind the Chieftain, their

eyes glowing blue. "It's time. We can sense the vibrations in the ground. They're coming."

Arryn sighed before looking to Cathillian. He gave her a gentle smile, and she turned back to the twins and nodded. "I guess you're up."

A dark smile crossed both their faces as they walked forward, easily crossing over the makeshift creek. The girls stood there, their bare feet planted on the ground, shoulder-width apart, and their hands raised to shoulder-height. Their heads were slightly bowed, and Arryn could sense only the subtlest of magic emanating from them.

They're tracking vibrations.

Watching them in action, even though they hadn't really done anything, Arryn couldn't help but be fascinated. Though she was worried about the travel, and even more worried about what they would run into in a land she had never been to, she couldn't help but be excited to see and learn new things.

Cathillian was right. She sure as hell wanted to see what these girls were made out of.

Off in the distance, the first line in Alaric's army showed themselves, and the girls dropped their hands, their heads raising. Once again, every movement they made was in tandem. They seemed to be connected at the mind, moving in unison, as if they were the same person, though neither one of them had any mental magic abilities.

Without warning, shouts began to ring out. The girls stomped their right foot forward, dropping down and slamming their right fist to the ground before rising into what reminded Arryn of the warrior yoga pose Zoe had tried to teach her.

As the twins lifted their arms, the earth shook, and a wall of packed earth rose that was wide enough to shield the immediate people behind them. Arryn could hear the sound of several tiny explosions on the other side, and knew it was the magitech rifles.

Those shots would have hit every one of them, had it not been for the twins.

She turned to Cathillian. "Okay, I stand corrected."

"What now?" the Chieftain asked. He had agreed to allow the twins the first go, so this part of the show was all theirs.

"Hold," Bast said flatly.

They held the warrior pose: all their weight on that front leg, bent at the knee, left leg stretched out behind them, one arm aimed straight in front of them, while the other pointed straight back. Their heads lowered again as they focused on the vibrations.

Arryn could hear the slightest rustle of leaves over the wall, and she knew the shadow warriors had returned.

Without saying a word, the girls snapped their heads up and the arms pointing behind them swung forward. Their hands clapped, and a thunderous *boom* echoed in front of them as the wall exploded into hundreds of thousands of pieces, blowing forward and taking out several men in the front line.

In front were the mercenaries, which didn't surprise Arryn at all. The men behind called out their battle cries as they rushed forward, jumping over their fallen friends. The twins lowered their bodies and then jumped straight into the air; Arryn's eyes widened as she watched them clear more than twenty feet. They slammed down hard on the ground, creating vibrations that shook the men, and knocked several in front off balance.

Cleo turned and looked behind her, her eyes blue. Arryn could see her panting, and knew they had expended way more energy than they should have. "Now!" Cleo called out.

CHAPTER TWENTY-ONE

Arryn ran forward, but Snow was faster. She leapt over Arryn, rushing the first man she saw. His eyes widened, a scream forming in his throat, before Snow clamped down hard on his head and squeezed with her powerful jaws. Arryn could hear the sickening crunch as his head exploded in her mouth, and the tiger dropped him to the ground, moving on to the next.

Animals that were under the control of the dark druids were attacking her friends and their familiars all over. Snow rushed forward to take several out, which she hated, because the animals were innocent. They didn't want to do their bidding, but they were forced. Fighting their influence was far more painful than death.

From what Arryn could see, as the battle raged on, the dark druids were beginning to lose some of their control; many animals were starting to flee.

Grabbing her bow, Arryn called for Snow and jumped on her back. They raced forward, zigzagging out of the way of attackers as Arryn did her best to thin the crowd. She took shot after shot, each one hitting her target. She had improved her technique while riding tiger-back, having practiced on horses.

The crowd began to thicken as more bandits rushed forward, and Arryn and Snow raced back to the makeshift creek. Arryn jumped down, hearing a loud grunt to her right, and a man fell at her feet, a knife in the back of his head. She looked up to see Celine making her way over.

"Boy, look who's come a long way," Arryn said with a smile.

Celine laughed. "You know it. How about we make use of this water?"

"I was thinking that myself," she agreed, her eyes flashing black.

Celine's eyes changed as well, and both women turned toward the water as Snow ran off to join the battle once again, making sure to keep the enemy out of reach of her master. Arryn heard a loud growl, and she looked over to see Dante taking down a would-be attacker.

"Good boy!" Arryn praised him as she lifted her hands.

Water began to lift from the creek, and the women froze it in tiny shards.

Arryn felt the searing pain before she heard the sound.

A magitech rifle blast had cut straight through her shoulder. She yelled out, grinding her teeth as blood began to pour down both her chest and back from the wound.

Looking ahead, she saw a wall of men holding magitech rifles and coming straight for them. She screamed loudly as she took a step forward, thrusting her hands out. Ice shards whistled through the air, impaling some; other men threw out a blast of telekinetic energy, shooting the ice right back at her.

Celine reacted quickly. A shield exploded around them and blocked the ice. As the men readied their weapons again, Arryn lifted her hands, raising water from the creek and freezing it into a solid wall. She dropped to the ground, yanking Celine down with her.

Ice chunks exploded all over as the men shot at the wall, approaching slowly and still firing.

Arryn drew on her nature magic and healed her shoulder. "Keep this shield solid," she ordered Celine.

Celine nodded, and Arryn threw her arm straight up to the sky. A vine unwound from the tree and wrapped around her waist before quickly pulling her up into the canopy. Once she was concealed inside, the vine fell away, and she could see the shadow warriors with their glowing green eyes.

"How about we have some fun?" Arryn asked, as blind shots from the magitech rifles began to shoot up through the trees.

It was Alehah that answered. "Absolutely."

Arryn smiled and nodded. "Good, keep my ass from hitting the ground."

Alehah stood straight and nodded only a second before Arryn jumped, diving headfirst toward the ground. When she was nearly ten feet from plummeting to the earth, vines whipped around each of her feet and legs individually, just as she grabbed the magitech rifle out of a mercenary's hand and smashed him in the face with the end of it.

Before they could retaliate, Alehah pulled Arryn back high into the tree, the vines falling away again.

"Stand back!" Arryn shouted.

All *Schatten* warriors in the tree backed against the trunk, where they were less likely to be hit. Down below, Arryn heard a war cry before she heard a heavy *thump*, and she knew Samuel was there to save the day.

There was no mistaking his screams in battle. That wasn't going to stop her from saving his short ass from getting killed in the process of trying to save Celine, who probably didn't need saving anyway.

Arryn nodded toward Alehah once again before running to the end of the branch and taking a dive. This time, she jumped much farther out, which allowed Alehah's vines to move her in an arc.

She swung down, shooting the pilfered rifle and taking out

two fighters before swinging it like a stick to take out a third. Just as before, Alehah yanked her back into the tree before they could get a steady shot on her.

"Step back!" Arryn said, everyone once again backing against the thick trunk.

Arryn stepped forward, putting her hands in front of her and slowly parting the leaves, willing the branches to separate just enough to allow her to see below. She whipped her head back just in time to dodge a shot; by the time she looked back, Samuel had already swung his hammer into the man's chest and was delivering the final blow to his head.

Arryn looked over to Alehah and smiled. "Thanks for the fun!"

Arryn used the vines that were still wrapped around her legs, to wrap around her waist before jumping down, carefully lowering herself the rest of the way so she wasn't injured.

She rushed forward and roundhouse-kicked a man in the face as he went after Samuel. He rounded on her and lifted his weapon, but she kicked the end of it, knocking it upward before she charged him, taking him down to the ground. His arms went out at his sides as he landed hard on the ground with Arryn on top of him.

As he tried to correct himself, Arryn pulled a ram's horn dagger from her belt as she brought her head down, breaking his nose. As she lifted her head, she stabbed him in the side of the throat. Then she willed the vine that had lowered her to take the magitech rifle into the canopy.

BAST AND CLEO had used quite a lot of energy in the beginning of the battle, but they weren't out entirely. Off in the distance, they could see Arryn diving in and out of the tree, taking men out left and right.

"She's kind of awesome," Bast said as she stopped a man mid-run with a punch to the face. His entire face collapsed under the force of the impact, and he fell dead to the ground.

"She's playing in the trees," Cleo said, picking a large branch up off the ground and swinging hard, taking down three men at once. "She's pretty awesome, but we have yet to see what she's really capable of. Let's hold our praises until she's showed us her cards. She's seen ours, we still need to see hers."

Cleo ran toward a group setting in on the Chieftain. Her eyes flashed blue as she forced power down to her legs and jumped. Just as before, she landed hard in front of the Chieftain, and the blast of energy that was forced outward in a large circle, threw ten men back.

"It's amazing what physical magic can do," the Chieftain said.

"I got more where that came from," she promised. Despite her confident words, she was feeling the extreme fatigue, and the Chieftain could see it all over her.

A man ran straight for her, and she focused the power in her arm and hand. She caught him by the throat, lifting him in the air with one hand before slamming him down on the ground and squeezing, effectively crushing his windpipe. She stood and turned toward the Chieftain, who was now staring at her with wide eyes.

"You know, it's funny. As far as natural physical strength goes, I can barely do my own hair some days without my arms hurting."

The Chieftain burst out laughing before whipping his staff around, hitting a man directly in the face and throwing him back to the ground.

"What about you, old man? Bast and I are curious enough to see what Arryn has to offer, but I'm betting you're hiding a lot under that grey hair."

Alexander smiled as his eyes flashed bright, neon green. Thunder cracked overhead, and the sky grew dark. Cleo's eyes widened as the wind began to blow. Her hair, even in braids, stood out as the charge in the air grew.

The Chieftain lifted his staff to the sky, and lightning bolts crashing down all around. He took down all the men that were struggling to stand from Cleo's attack, and several more that had approached. They all sprawled out on the ground, dead.

He turned toward her with a smile on his face, but it quickly fell as he whipped his staff around, knocking her legs out from under her. She was about to ask what the hell he had just done, when a blast of wind blew, and she peered back in time to see two approaching men fly backward onto their asses.

The Chieftain stepped forward and extended his hand. She smiled and took it to stand. "Thanks, old man."

"You saved me first, young woman. Now, let's go find my old friend, Alaric, shall we?"

CATHILLIAN NARROWLY MISSED a swipe from one of Snow's massive paws as she attacked one man before going on to another. Most of the men ran when they saw her coming for them, but some thought they were crafty enough to outsmart her.

That will never be the case.

Cathillian sliced his sword downward, managing to dodge a blast from a magitech rifle before bringing the sword up again and slashing the mercenary across the face. The man screamed out just as Samuel took the final blow.

"Well, there you are!" Cathillian said. "I was wondering where my best little friend was."

Samuel laughed. "And I was wonderin' where me skinny ogre friend had gone to."

Cathillian gave him an offended expression before stepping back and throwing an elbow into the face of one of the bandits, knocking him down before running his sword through his chest.

"Now, I'm surely not *that* ugly, am I?" Cathillian asked as he turned back to Samuel.

Samuel swung his hammer and knocked the legs out from under one bandit as Cathillian pulled the knife from his belt and threw it, stabbing another in the face.

"Come on," Cathillian said. "You know you think I'm pretty."

"Yeah, lad. Yer just the girl fer me," Samuel said with a sarcastic tone, grunting as he took another swing.

"See? I told you!" Cathillian charged to his left, jumping up and wrapping his legs around a bandit's head before flipping himself backward, the momentum taking the man to the ground. He twisted his hips, effectively breaking the man's neck.

"If you plan to marry me, you might have to fight Arryn for it," Cathillian said with a grunt as he stood.

Samuel laughed. "Lad, I'm pretty sure she'd sell ye fer a half pint of the shite rearick brew. Not even the good stuff."

Cathillian laughed as he ran over and grabbed the knife he had thrown earlier, pulling it from the man's eyes socket. "I'd guess you're probably right about that."

A knife came out of nowhere, whizzing right past Cathillian's head and stabbing into the throat of the man that had been coming after him. They both turned and saw Celine standing there, hands on her hips.

"Are the two of you ladies seriously going to stand around and flirt all day? I don't know if I can continuously save you damsels in distress," Celine said.

Samuel's face turned red as he shook his head. "I'll be good."

Celine pointed behind Cathillian, and he nodded. He quickly turned and stomped his foot outward, breaking the knee of the approaching enemy before slicing upward with his sword, scoring a fatal gash from left hip to right shoulder.

He turned back to Celine and smiled. "I'll be good, too."

She sighed and shook her head. "Glad to hear it. We have to find Arryn before she does anything crazy. Elysia said she hasn't seen Alaric *or* Jerick, and she's worried Arryn will go after them *alone*."

"Would Elysia even know 'em if she saw 'em?" Samuel asked.

Cathillian snorted. "My mom knew them when she was a kid. She may have been a toddler at the time, but her brain is like a steel trap—she never forgets a face."

They all turned, about to head back toward the creek where they had last seen Arryn, when two explosions sounded in quick succession.

CHAPTER TWENTY-TWO

Alaric stood in the middle of the battle, watching everything fall apart around him. He looked down, his eyes widening as he stared into the cold, dead eyes of Locke, the very man who was supposed to be the best of the best.

At least, that was what *he* had said. *Obviously, he was wrong.*

Alaric smiled. "Sorry, Locke. I guess when we succeed without you, we won't be going to the Heights after all. Thanks for your sacrifice. It will be promptly forgotten, I assure you."

Jerick ran up, out of breath. "Brother, I hate to say this, but this is a lost cause. Alexander is too strong. His people..." He looked around, watching everyone locked in combat. "Alexander has always been more powerful than either one of us. That was *years* ago. These people are even stronger than Alexander was when we left decades ago. So, how the hell strong is he *now*? And we've seen what Arryn can do..."

Alaric's nostrils flared as he became angrier by the second. Alexander had always bested him; he wasn't about to let him do it again. At the very least, if he lost, he was taking Alexander out with him. But he wanted Arryn first. Alaric wanted to deliver her dead body to Alexander, wanted to see the look of absolute horror on his face when he realized he had lost his best champion.

Looking down, Alaric kicked Locke's body over and retrieved his pack, which contained four magitech grenades. He slung it over his shoulders and smiled at his brother.

"What are you doing?" Jerick asked. "Didn't you hear me? We have to leave. *Now*. Leave the rest of them. They don't matter now."

Alaric shook his head. "Follow me into battle, brother. We don't have to fight for long. We only have to deliver the contents of this bag to Alexander and Arryn. Let's take out as many of them as we can and *then* flee. We can run east into the Valley. They won't expect us to go there."

Alaric watched his brother's expression lighten from irritation to understanding. Finally, Jerick nodded. "As you wish, brother. Let's do this together."

Alaric nodded and began walking toward the enemy. He sensed a life force from above just as it descended upon him. His eyes flashed as he lifted his hand, looking up into the terrified eyes of a woman, dangling from the tree as she clutched at her chest. Her magic failed; the vine went limp and dumped her to the ground, snapping her neck on impact.

They continued moving forward. Jerick whipped his hand out to the side, and vines tightened around another druid's neck hard enough to crush her larynx. They moved through with confidence, going around the outside of the battle and picking up speed.

It took some time, but they were able to make it around the majority of the fighting, only having to take down stragglers or shadow warriors as they dropped from the trees.

Then there she was. *Arryn*.

She took two rapid back-to-back shots with her bow before slinging the weapon over her shoulder and running forward, jumping into the air, and mule kicking a man in the chest before tumbling over backward to land on her feet.

She knelt, whipping the bow from her shoulder again before grabbing an arrow that had fallen to the ground in her assault. She took aim, shot, then immediately nocked another fallen arrow.

"She is brilliant," Jerick said. "It really *is* a shame we have to kill her."

Alaric snorted. "I'd give my right arm to have that woman by my side. She's fearless and powerful—but she'll never give in."

Alaric took the bag from his shoulder and reached inside, handing his brother one of the magitech grenades.

ARRYN HAD RETRIEVED her bow and was doing her best to thin out more of the mercenaries and dark druids as they rushed forward in groups. She had watched many of her druid friends go down, but they were *winning*. The battle would soon be over, and she still had yet to find Alaric and Jerick.

Before this war could be considered truly over and finished, the dark Chieftains *had* to die.

They would stop at *nothing* to have the Dark Forest. Now that she knew they were capable of hiring mercenaries and using magitech weaponry, she would put nothing past them. Too many lives had been lost, and she refused to risk losing any more.

Something sharp pierced through her back, straight through her abdomen. She looked down to see a sword jutting out. She heard a familiar scream before the sword was swiftly—and painfully—pulled out. She clutched at her side, turning around. There was no one behind her except enemies fighting other druids.

She looked up just in time to watch a body fall from the trees with a sword run through the chest. She peered up again to see

Corrine dropping down just behind him, a vine wrapped around her waist and eyes glowing bright green.

Arryn's eyes widened. "What the hell are you doing here? You're supposed to be with Zoe and the other children!"

Corrine reached out and touched Arryn, heat immediately rushing through her as she healed her wound.

"I couldn't let anything happen to you. I know I can't fight down here with you, but I'm fast and I'm good in the trees. I'm *not* going back, not until I know this is over and all of you are safe."

Arryn felt the presence of someone quickly approaching from behind, and she pulled the sword from the chest of the man Corrine had killed before turning and bringing it down on her new opponent's leg. She pulled back and swung again, decapitating him.

"*Shit!*" she shouted before turning back to face Corrine. "I didn't mean to do that. I didn't want you to see that."

Corrine looked down at the body at her feet, and then again at Arryn.

"Was that the first enemy you've ever taken down?" Arryn asked, her voice a bit softer.

Corrine nodded as Arryn grabbed a ram's horn dagger from her belt, pulled it back, and threw it hard over Corrine's head to hit a man in the chest. Her eyes flashed black as she telekinetically pulled it back, not wanting to lose that one, like she had the other one, earlier in battle.

"Yes, it was," Corrine said. "I'm sorry, okay! I'm not disturbed or broken by it. You have *no* idea how much death I've seen. At least all this is for a purpose. This is to save our *home*. Our *family*. Jerick did it for fun, for torture. I promise I'll stay out of the way, but I'm staying close enough to heal you if you need it."

Corrine tilted her head to the side, pointing behind Arryn. The warrior's eyes flashed black as she turned, throwing a hand out and sending the man flying back several feet before hitting the ground, his head smashing on a tree root.

"I don't have time to argue with you about this. Get your ass in the trees, and stay high enough you can't be seen. Don't you *dare* come down. I don't care if a sword goes through me again. Got it?"

Corrine nodded once before the vine pulled her back up.

"I'll keep her safe!" Alehah called down.

Arryn sighed, shaking her head. "That kid is gonna be the death of me."

Taking a deep breath, she charged forward, rushing back into battle. She sensed familiar dark energy and stopped in her tracks. She turned her head, her eyes widening as they came to rest on Alaric. The world was going to hell around him, his men dying one right after another, but he still held a confident expression.

That disturbed her. As she took a step forward, a dark smile crossed his face. Her heart skipped a beat, knowing something terrible was about to happen.

Is he capable of using his death touch on this many people? Can he use it on me from that far away?

He lifted his hand, and she recognized the metal he held, though she didn't recognize the shape. It was the same kind of casing that Waylon and Elon had used on the magitech mines. He held it out to the side, his thumb directly in the air as he pressed down, his smile growing. He pulled back his hand, and she knew he was about to throw it.

"*Everybody down!*" Arryn shouted, flexing her entire body as she let a blast of telekinetic energy explode around her, throwing as many people as she could out of the way. She barely had enough time to raise a shield around herself before the explosion went off.

She flew backward, hitting a tree, her head slamming against it with great force. She fell to the ground, unable to breathe. Another explosion went off, and she saw large fireballs engulfing trees and people. A scream wrenched the air, and she realized it was hers as she struggled to pull herself forward.

Inhaling was difficult, and she used what little power she had to inspect her body. She could feel debris inside her. Within a few moments, she could tell they were tiny metal pieces, more than likely from whatever it was he had thrown.

Though Elon's mines relied mostly on charges and the energy from amphorald crystals, she knew from at least one conversation with him that he had thought about using little spherical or jagged metal pieces; something he learned had been in similar weapons long ago.

As her power waned, she couldn't muster enough to heal herself, and her eyes began to flutter closed. The last thing she saw was Corrine trying to drop down from the tree, and Alehah yanking her back up before she could be seen by anyone who would do her harm.

PAIN RADIATED through Arryn as she opened her eyes, the very act of breathing bringing agony like she had never experienced—though she wouldn't know that.

As she looked around, she had no idea where she was or what she was looking at. There were bodies all around, but it didn't make sense. It was as though a fog had settled in.

It's all a dream.

As she made her way through the forest, her ears ringing and her eyes wandering over the death and destruction, she found herself intrigued, though not scared.

Weak hands reached out for her, but she walked past, not understanding why. The sounds of crying echoed through her ears, but she couldn't be sure if it had been that or the ringing twisting to make her believe it had been screams.

It didn't matter. It would all be over soon.

There wasn't a tree that looked familiar, nor a face. Nothing there was real, and she had no way of knowing just how long she had traveled. She came upon a river and wandered around its bank.

Several times she had to wipe blood away from her face and eyes. She was covered in it, but couldn't understand why or where it had come from. Then, as the ringing slowly began to dissipate, she heard someone yelling.

It was so peaceful here, why would anyone want to scream?

"Arryn!" The sound came again, only this time she made out the word.

Turning, she looked around, but saw nothing. The action made her feel a little dizzy, and she laughed as she stumbled over to a large rock by the river bank.

"Arryn!" The voice had completely broken through the ringing now, and she saw a man stepping out of the forest and walking toward her.

Who is he, and why was he shouting at me?

"Arryn!" he said, his voice taking on a relieved tone now instead of the frantic one he'd had before. As she looked at him with total confusion, his relief fell from his expression, a look of worry replacing it. "Arryn?"

She laughed again, pointing at the man who seemed terribly worried about someone named Arryn. "I..." She coughed, realizing the smoke had done more to her throat than she had thought. But she would wake soon, so it didn't matter. "I don't know who that is. You have the wrong person."

The man stared at her, his long blonde hair blowing slightly in the breeze. He began to shake his head a bit as he stepped closer. "*You* are Arryn."

Her smile fell as he began to approach her. She had no idea who he was, and he was much larger than she was. There were knives on his belt, and blood on his clothes and even his hands. There were even a few drops on his face.

At that moment, she thought back to the dead bodies she had seen littering the area she had awoken in.

"It was you! You hurt them." The thought had occurred to her to run away, but why? She wanted to see where the dream went.

The man's eyes flashed green, earning a gasp out of the young woman before he said, "I'm sorry to do this, but it's for your own safety."

Dream or not, she didn't want to stick around to see what he meant by that.

She tried to move quickly, but he was much faster. Vines shot out from the ground, wrapping her from her elbows down to her ankles. They held her tight, keeping her from moving at all.

The man made his move then, running up and placing his hands on either side of her face. His hands were large, and very warm. Something about that warmth felt familiar as it raced through her entire body.

And then everything began to change. She didn't like this, not at all. Suddenly, she was painfully aware that her ribs had been crushed, and was now aware of the splitting headache she had. She began to see memories flashing through her mind, explosions in the forest, and then she became aware of even more.

It's not a dream... It's not a dream at all.

Within moments, though it seemed like an eternity, her ribs cracked back into place, her headache dissipated, and she took her first painless breath.

"Is it you?" he asked cautiously. "Do you know where you are? What happened?"

She slowly nodded, her expression reflecting the rage that was coming back with all of her other emotions now that her broken mind had been healed. "Get me a fucking healer. I need to be at full capacity. I made a promise to Alaric, and I'm about to make good on it."

CHAPTER TWENTY-THREE

Cathillian was quick to grab whatever healers he could find who weren't occupied with others injured in the blasts. Corrine showed up just as five healers finished shoving as much power into Arryn as they could without depleting themselves for others.

Combining power among several druids seemed to lessen the overall amount of magic used for any single person. Those healers would now be able to go help others with little negative effect.

"Corrine, I need you to go back to the village. Those blasts could've easily gone into the trees. Do you have *any* idea how many pieces of metal came out of me?" Arryn asked as she saw Corrine walking onto the beach.

"But the blast *didn't* go into the trees. I'm fine, and I kept my promise. I told you, I'm not leaving until I know you're safe."

Arryn stood, her face turning red as she became angry. "Do you not realize that *I'm* the adult? Do you not realize *I'm* responsible for *you*? If anything happens to you, I will never forgive myself as long as I live. And in case ya hadn't noticed, nature magic users live for a *very* long time."

Corrine recoiled a bit at Arryn's harshness, but then she pushed her chin up, balled her fists, and took a few steps forward. "You need me!"

"Of course, I do!" Arryn shouted. "I love you, dammit! Don't you realize that? You're like my own child. I will *always* need you. But you're eight… years… old. You need to be a kid for as long as we can let that happen. I can't have you out on the battlefield and going on adventures, risking your life."

"*Arryn,*" Elysia warned. Her voice was soft, but Arryn heard the edge in it. She looked over, anger still on her face, though the older woman's was surprisingly gentle. "Be easy."

"'Going out on adventures'…" Corrine said. "Does that mean you don't want me to go with you when you leave the Dark Forest?"

Tears filled Arryn's eyes. "This is a conversation that we can have later. Right now, we need to find the dark Chieftains."

"No!" Corrine shouted. "I'm having this conversation now! I saved your life! *Twice.* How the hell do you think you survived that blast?"

Arryn was taken aback by Corinne's fierceness and cursing.

"I moved through the trees without anyone seeing me. I couldn't drop down because I was terrified. I admit it. I was too scared to get down on the ground. I knew that if they saw me, there was *no* way you'd survive. They would've killed me, and you would have died, too. I couldn't touch you, so I healed you as best I could from the tree branches. It wasn't much, but it was enough to stop the heaviest bleeding."

Arryn's brows furrowed as she looked at Corrine with shock and admiration. "You did that?"

"It seems she has a talent for healing," the Chieftain said. "When she first healed you from a distance in the dark druid camp, I thought she would make an incredible healer—but then she showed such promise in the pit. It seems she is a young woman of many talents. Alaric can do the death touch from a distance, and it seems she can heal from a distance."

"You need me," Corrine repeated her words from earlier.

Arryn nodded. "I do, but right now—"

The girl shook her head. "No. You plan to go after them, don't you?"

She nodded. "I do, which is why—"

"Which is exactly why you need me," Corrine interrupted again. "When you went down, I saw them take off. They're heading east. Jerick is pulling them through the trees; Snow won't be fast enough to catch up to them."

Arryn opened her mouth, but Elysia interrupted.

"We always encourage everyone to do what they feel is right," Elysia reminded her. "We would never consider putting a child in the middle of a battle, but she's here, and she's been very useful. If she stays in the trees, she will stay out of harm's way. If she believes she can do it, let her try. Because I'll be honest... We don't have the strength to propel you through the trees fast enough, and neither do the *Schatten*. We will have to take famil-iars, and if you use that much power yourself, you'll be useless in battle. If you take Snow, you might risk losing her. You're the only one of us with the energy to end this fight."

Corrine smiled triumphantly. "In other words, I'm all you got."

Arryn laughed, unable to believe just how strong-willed this child was. Finally, she said, "Again, keep your ass in the trees. Don't come down for *any* reason. Don't let them see you." She turned to the rest of them. "All of you get there as fast as you possibly can. I don't know what I'll be capable of, but in case this goes badly, you need to be there."

The Chieftain nodded. "Trust me, I wouldn't miss this for the world."

She nodded and then looked down to Corrine. "By the way, your ass is grass when we get back."

"Yeah, I kinda figured," Corrine said with a smile.

CHAPTER TWENTY-FOUR

Corrine's eyes glowed bright, neon green. Her legs were wrapped around Arryn's waist as she rode piggyback through the trees. Her arms moved freely as she controlled the vines. One was wrapped around them both that kept her firmly tethered to Arryn as she continued to work her magic on others that propelled them from one tree to the next.

But Arryn could feel Corrine's energy waning; she didn't have much left.

It didn't take long for them to make it from the river all the way across to the eastern side of the woods. Arryn knew they would soon run into Alaric and Jerick, and she began to get nervous, hoping she would have enough energy left to do what she needed to do.

If they were as strong as the Chieftain, she stood no chance.

Arryn's eyes flashed green as she opened up her senses to all life in the immediate area. She didn't want to search a very wide radius, wasting her energy in the process, so she kept close.

As they neared the eastern edge of the forest, Arryn sensed the dark Chieftains. They had just exited the forest and were now forced to run on foot.

Corrine swung them one last time, high into the last tree at the very edge before dropping her magic. All the vines fell, and she climbed down, darkness settling in around her eyes with magically-induced exhaustion. "This is it. Are you ready?" she asked as she stepped down onto a thick branch.

Arryn nodded, her eyes never leaving her targets. "Oh, I'm very ready. I'm going to kill Jerick for everything he did to you, and I'm going to kill Alaric for everything he did to my father."

Corrine wrapped her arms around Arryn, pulling her tight into a hug. "I love you, too," the girl said, responding to what Arryn had said before they left.

Arryn leaned down and kissed the top of her head. "Remember. Stay high in the trees. Much higher than this."

Corrine only nodded before Arryn jumped down to the ground.

Her eyes flashing black and green, she charged forward as fast as she could. She made a mental note to ask Bast and Cleo how they channeled their magic the way they did. She was much better with nature magic than she was with physical magic.

Arryn watched as Jerick came to a hard stop, turning and whipping his hands out, vines bursting from the ground. Both of her hands shot out, telekinetic energy gripping the vines and ripping them out of the ground as she continued to run.

Vines began bursting from the ground all over, and she had to work hard to dodge them, unable to use that much physical magic this soon. One grabbed her, and she whipped her blade out before it lifted from the ground, cutting it and continuing to move.

Alaric turned, his eyes flashing as his hands lifted in front of him. Arryn immediately felt the hard thump in her chest as her heart struggled to beat. She felt her energy draining, and knew it was the death touch.

Thirty feet. That's all I have to go.

"You should have joined us when you had the chance," Alaric

said with a smile on his face. "You know, I thought I killed you with the grenades, but it turns out I get to kill you twice. Though, this time it'll be a bit more *permanent*."

Arryn closed her eyes, focusing on everything around her as she meditated, doing her best to relax and cast magic at the same time. She could feel her healing abilities warring against his death touch, but she could also feel him struggling to hold it.

She was too far away, and he had already expended too much energy.

At that moment, she knew she only had to last a few moments longer. She cleared her mind, drowning out his pointless threats as she focused on continuously healing herself.

Thunder cracked overhead, and the sky began to blacken. Shadows fell over everything, and Arryn knew this storm was the Chieftain's creation. He and the others were getting close, and she quickly realized she wasn't the only one who had taken notice...

Alaric dropped his magic, and Arryn opened her eyes. She saw him frantically looking around, realizing Alexander was coming. He was terrified. As she struggled to stand, the look of fear on his face evoked a volcano of emotion inside of her.

For years, my father feared for his life, while this asshole stood over him and laughed and took joy in his pain. Her eyes narrowed as she focused a death stare at him. *He doesn't get to be afraid of someone else. It's* me *he needs to be afraid of.*

Arryn stood, her eyes flashing black, as the ground began to gently rumble under her feet.

"Brother, we have bigger problems than Alexander right now. Focus," Jerick said pointing to Arryn.

Vines again burst out of the ground behind her, wrapping around her throat, and Jerick threw his other hand out, a blast of wind hitting her in the chest and knocking her back as he continued to choke her. She lifted her knife and cut the vine away, taking a deep breath and coughing as she rolled over to her hands and knees to climb to her feet.

As she did, she saw the others just reaching the edge of the forest, Bast and Cleo among them. She looked overhead at the storm clouds that had been brewing and smiled. Alexander, her Chieftain, had conjured that storm, so it wouldn't take much of her energy at all to use it.

She turned, watching both of the dark Chieftains run like cowards. She raised her hand to the sky, sending lightning bolts raining down in a wall to stop them in their tracks. They tried to run in a different direction, and she whipped her hand around, a wall of wind throwing them back.

She continued to advance, slowly stalking her way toward them. "What's wrong? Ready to leave so soon?"

Both the Chieftains stood there, panicking as they debated what to do. They looked to the sky, each of them peering around Arryn. Jerick lifted his hands again, but she flicked her wrist, and telekinetic energy pulled his arm out of the socket; she repeated the process on the other side. Screams erupted as he fell to his knees.

She laughed. "You really are afraid of him, aren't you?" Her irises began to turn green as the white parts turned even blacker. The storm clouds began to dissipate as the bright skies returned. "There you go, ladies. Now you can focus on me because *I'm* the one you need be afraid of. I made a promise to you, do you remember, Alaric?"

She came to a stop roughly twenty feet away, knowing his death touch was no longer a worry. If he even attempted to use it again, he would go down before she did—though she didn't have much left, either.

She could see the look of disdain on his face as he slowly nodded his head. "You said that you would send me to hell."

With a very wide smile, she said, "You know, I *always* make good on my promises."

Alaric shook his head. "If you think this fight is your last, you're wrong. We only brought a fraction of Locke's men. There were hundreds more down there. His wife is even worse than he was. She'll come for you. I can help you."

Arryn laughed, throwing her head back a little before focusing back in on him and shaking her head. "You can't even help *yourself*. If you think for a second I'm going to let either one of you live after what you've done, you have never been more mistaken in your life. Jerick, the justice I seek is for Corrine. For the torture you delivered to her—a child—over the course of her entire life. Alaric, your crimes are far too many to list. Your death will be justice for many, but for me, it will be specifically for my father."

As her voice became more heated—they no doubt sensed their end coming, along with her increasing rage—their eyes flashed. But she only smiled.

She spread her legs shoulder-width apart, thrusting her hand downward. A blast of physical energy hit the ground hard enough for a massive crack to form between her feet. As she focused on it, the earth quaked even more, splitting it even further.

"I should have killed your father the day Aeris brought him to me. Instead, I just told Aeris to beat the shit out of him," Alaric said.

Even hearing it sent her further into a rage, Jerick obviously taking notice and quickly turning and begging him to run. Unfortunately for Jerick, Alaric had accepted the inevitable.

Arryn brought her hands out to her sides, massive chunks of dirt and rock lifting from the ground as it continued to shake. The crack grew exponentially, traveling directly between the brothers.

"You're going to spend eternity right here in this very spot, never able to return to the Dark Forest, forced to live in the Arcadian Valley that you hated *so* very much. For your crimes, you're sentenced to die. And yes, I'm sending your fucking asses to hell—*your* version of it."

Arryn's entire body flexed as even more rock and earth exploded from the ground, everything around them shaking as it knocked the dark Chieftains off balance and threw them into the chasm. She heard them screaming as she brought her hands down, all that dirt and rock slamming back down to the ground and crushing them inside.

She no longer heard them, and she could sense the moment their life forces ended. Now that they were gone, her entire body wavered, and she had to catch her balance. She wasn't nearly as weak as she had been when leaving the dark druid encampment, but she was certainly close to collapsing.

Had it not been for the healing she had received before engaging them in battle, she never would have been able to survive that.

Everyone rushed to her side, pulling her into hugs and kissing her face. Cathillian grabbed her and kissed her before pulling her against his chest and holding her for several moments.

"By the way," Arryn said, her voice weak. "According to Alaric, we didn't get so lucky with the bandits. We killed their leader, but he said there are more. A lot more. I'm not sure how accurate that is, but at least we know the possibility."

"Shh. Let's not worry about that right now. If he meant it, we'll deal with it when we get there. If not, then we can move on to Kemet," Cathillian said.

Arryn yawned as he picked her up bride-style and carried her back toward the forest. Snow made her way out, Corrine riding on Dante.

"Look who's finally big enough for me to ride!" Corrine said excitedly.

Arryn laughed. "Glad to hear it. Seems you needed a good mount when the time came, anyway. When you find your own familiar, it's hard to say if he or she will be bigger, or change in other ways. So, at least you know you'll have Dante to ride."

"I have my baby wolf! Reaper. He might be my familiar one day, and then I can ride him," Corrine said.

Arryn tapped Cathillian's shoulder, and he let her down. She straightened her mess of a shirt and made her way over to Snow on steady feet.

"Hey," Cathillian said. "I thought you were all weak and stuff."

She shrugged and smiled. "Actually, I just wobbled a bit. You're the one that picked me up and didn't bother to ask. You just *assumed* I was weak. You underestimated me."

He laughed. "Well, historically speaking, the majority of times I find you after you've been in a big battle, you've gone all lady balls out and have exhausted yourself."

"Point taken. I definitely need a nap. Like, a two-day nap and some food. That would be *great*," Arryn said.

Snow head-butted her arm, rubbing her cheek on Arryn's shoulder before kneeling down. Arryn climbed on and gave her scratches as she leaned forward, laying her face in the soft fur and snuggling in. She couldn't wait to get back to her cabin.

EPILOGUE

Several days passed, and everything in the Dark Forest was beginning to settle back in. Because of their quick planning, no children or elders in the village were injured during the battle. Zoe had done her job, and had done more than that. She had kept them protected, but also kept them calm.

Shortly after the celebration in Arryn's honor as well as the triumph over Alaric, Zoe said her goodbyes and headed back to the Heights with a group of ten well-trained warriors. With no worries about someone coming for the Dark Forest now, the Chieftain felt confident sending several along with her to make sure she made it home all right. Though Locke was dead, they knew the possibility of bandits roaming around in Arcadian Valley was still there.

Especially once Locke's wife discovered he wouldn't be returning. At least, if the dark Chieftain was to be believed.

Arryn asked Cathillian to send Echo to Arcadia with a letter for Amelia to let her know the war was over, and peace among the Arcadian's, the mystics, and the druids had finally been found. The Arcadian Valley was now a place of unity they had all said was in the design from the very beginning with Ezekiel. Now, life could begin the way the Founder had always meant for it to be.

The only thing standing in their way was the damn bandits, and Arryn intended to deal with them soon enough.

Amelia had sent back a letter letting them know Sven and Ren had arrived to request assistance because the murders had gotten worse. Julianne had also returned to the Temple, and Arryn knew she would soon hear of what had transpired from Zoe upon her return.

Though Arryn was enjoying her time relaxing with everyone with no worries of anyone coming for them, she knew that time was coming to an end.

Even if the large number of bandits south of the Heights didn't exist, they would still have to leave to go to Kemet and save Bast and Cleo's people.

"When are you guys planning to head out?" Elysia asked as Arryn stood from the fire, preparing to go back to her cabin.

Arryn exhaled deeply, shaking her head. "Honestly, I'm not ready. But I can't just sit by and let innocent people suffer. We still need time to prepare, so I would say within forty-eight hours."

"Have you thought any more about Corrine?" Elysia asked.

"I'm conflicted. What do you think I should do? I want to take her, because I don't want her feel like I've abandoned her, but I'm so worried," Arryn said, her eyes momentarily flashing black as she conjured a fireball and threw it into the fire pit. It roared back to life.

"Personally, I think you should take her with you. Yes, it might be dangerous, but I think with all of you, she will be just fine. Not only that, but if she misses out on this journey, she might regret it. She might resent you. You were pretty strong when you initially left for Arcadia, but just how much stronger did you become while you were gone?"

She sighed as she nodded. Corrine walked past them, heading

toward her own cabin when Arryn rushed over to walk next to her.

"So, I was thinking," she said.

Corrine stopped, turning her beautiful face toward Arryn. "What about?"

"First off, thank you for saving me. I can't repay you for what you did. You saved my life twice, and helped me to bring peace to everyone here in the Dark Forest including my father, including you, and also including me. What you did drives me insane, and it makes me want to tie you up and lock you away. But it also makes me very proud. In the short time you've been here, you have grown incredibly fast."

Corrine smiled, the fire lighting her face up just enough that Arryn could see the blush rise to her cheeks at the complements. "Thank you."

Arryn nodded. "After serious thought, and also after talking to Elysia—who is the smartest person I've ever met, and unfortunately the only mother-figure I've known for most of my life—I decided you should go with us when we leave."

Corinne's face lit up as a large smile grew. She leapt forward, wrapping her arms around Arryn and hugging her tight. She returned the hug, leaning down and laying her head on Corrine's.

"I won't let you down!" Corrine said.

Arryn smiled, her thumb brushing across the girl's cheek. "I know you won't. Now, go get some sleep. We leave in two days."

Without saying another word, the girl ran off to her cabin. Arryn turned and nearly ran directly into her father. Yet another person she was incredibly proud of. She had seen him fighting, using his favorite sword as he had long ago.

He had cut down dark druids left and right, taking them down with ease. It was true that he was rusty, and he wasn't nearly as good as he used to be, but he was still incredible. She knew that if he kept training, he would be just as strong as he once was.

"Two days, huh?" he asked.

She nodded. "Yep. Are you gonna be okay here without me?"

He smiled. "I hate to see you go, but I know that you have to. I know it's what you have to do. And even though I hate that you won't be around, I can't complain about it. I raised you to be strong and fight for the weak. I'm so proud of you."

She smiled as she hugged him. She'd had enough hugs the past three days to choke an antisocial person. Luckily for her, they were from people who mattered the most.

"It's getting late," he said. "You should take your own advice and get some rest. I know you slept for the last two days, but you still need it."

She smiled and nodded. "Good night, dad. I love you."

As she turned, heading toward her cabin, he said, "And Arryn?"

"Yeah?" she asked turning to face him.

"Kick their asses. They're Samuel's family and friends. Teach them why messing with good people is the worst sin a person can commit."

Arryn smiled. "Did you have any doubts?"

FINIS

Well, fancy seein' you here! Book SIX!!!! Yes! All of the exclamation points!!! I've been trying not to elicit any eye rolls or exasperated shakes of Michael's head while he reads them, so I have been cutting him some slack lately. *winks* Just kidding. He likes that we all joke about the e2p2 (excessive exclamation point problem) that I suffer from.

Anyway! How have all of you been? Do you know what? The reviews have been amazing to read, and I LOVE them! Thank you! All of you have been so generous with them, and I appreciate that deeply. Keep them coming! We love to hear from you (especially me—the make the days so exciting! Mostly when trying to power through and focus that day!), and we love them!

This time, instead of *ending* with your "review assignment"—I'm going to begin with it!

Given the date of release, I would love to know what holiday traditions you celebrate! I don't care if it's Christmas, or Hanukkah, or anything else. Or, if you don't have typical holiday traditions, is there something else that you like to do this time of year (big annual ice fishing trip, vacation spent reading, etc)?

Our holidays have been relatively the same for years, except that one time my dad randomly forgot like... ten or more years of traditions? No idea about that...

But since I was a kid, Thanksgiving Day was celebrated at others' houses. So, we would load up and go to my aunt's (because my grandmother Candy did *not* cook—she claimed you'd die if that happened. I never tested it... Though she could make some *awesome* bacon sammiches), or whoever was holding it that year on my mom's side. That sometimes changed from year to year.

But *Friday* was for us at home.

My parents were divorced, so my Dad always made his Thanksgiving on Friday. I always loved it. And my dad made the *best* lemon merengue pie. I always hated the merengue though, which he took as a personal insult. But then in later years, I started to like it. So, he liked me again. *laughs* When he remarried, he randomly forgot about years of tradition and actually said, "What? Why did you make plans for Thursday? We *always* do it on Thursday!"

Luckily, we were on the phone when having this conversation. The confused look on my face surely could have killed anyone who looked upon it. I inherited his forgetfulness. So, I get to look forward to doing this to my own children. Should be fun and interesting! Haha.

But now, since my younger sister, Amanda, was fortunate enough to buy her first home with her wonderful husband, Clint, she has it there every year, and let me just say, their Thanksgivings are *amazing*. She is an incredible hostess. Did *not* take after me ol' memaw Candy in that area at all! She would be proud.

For Christmas, we also go to my sister's house! She plays Christmas movies for everyone while they are waiting on dinner. Last year was Christmas Vacation, and I'm hoping that this year will be, too, because I love that movie and we've already watched my other favorite, Elf. Plus... this year, it is going to be SO very appropriate—and you're about to find out why. After dinner, we always open presents.

However, since I know there's exactly zero chance for her to read this before Christmas Eve, when I will be at her house, I wanted to share what I got for her. And yes… I will walk straight into their house and hand each one their gifts and expect them both to wear them/use them right at that moment.

I got my brother-in-law a shirt that has Chevy Chase's rant from National Lampoon's Christmas Vacation ("I want to look him straight in the eye, and I wanna tell him what a…"—that one) on it. It is riddled with all the curse words, and they aren't bleeped out. I'm going to hand it to him and make him change whatever he's wearing. It's on a normal red, men's tee-shirt. I grabbed it on Amazon for anyone reading this with wide eyes wanting their own to offend or humor the family with next year.

For my sister, I got a baseball jersey style shirt (white with black sleeves), and it also has a Christmas Vacation quote on it. It says, "Jolliest bunch of Assholes this side of the Nuthouse" on it.

Oh!!! And the best part? I completed it with the moose glasses —which I will also hand them when showing up. Yep. I bought the moose cups for them to drink their eggnog out of. I absolutely CANNOT wait for them to get those gifts! It'll be so fun! They *love* that movie, and my sister is a Christmas freak. She loves, loves, loves Christmas.

Thanks to LMBPN, KGU, and all of you amazing people, this year I was able to have a good Christmas for my kiddos and my sister, niece, and brother-in-law. I can't tell you just how exciting that is. It's been years, so I have a *lot* to be grateful for this year.

Also, this Christmas is extra special for me because I was able to buy back my childhood home. I've been working on that for almost two years now, and I was finally able to. I know this is an all-Christmas/holiday themed Author's Notes, but it's definitely that time of year for a lot of us! And remember… no matter what religion you are, what holiday you celebrate, or if you don't celebrate anything at all, I would love to know what you guys love to do around this time of year, too!

Thank you again for all your support and love. You guys are absolutely amazing! <3 <3 <3

Until next time! Happy reading, and Merry Christmas, Happy Holidays (no matter what that may be), and of course, Happy New Year!

-Candy

First, THANK YOU for not only reading this story, but allowing me a chance to provide an author notes without E2P2 issues. (Snicker!)

Now, if we have a book out in April, I might not be able to accomplish that act as April Fools would sorely tempt me to do a massive "I can out Candy...*Candy*" effort for the exclamation marks.

I will have to say that at fifty, and with the youngest two (the twins) JUST in their first year of college, I'm kinda ready to step away from massive Christmas seasons.

(I know, *BAH HUMBUG!*)

But, let me explain!

You see, our oldest is twenty-five this year. So, I've had twenty-five years of children and Christmas. Some of those years were sedate...Well, maybe two of them. Otherwise, you do what you can to make Christmas special for the kids and a couple were huge. Not because we had tons of money, but rather gifts were purchased all year long on specials as stores tried to get rid of toys (they were real young at this point).

So, when summer died down, and the stores had those squirtsoakers marked down from $25 to $5.99 they were SNAGGED and stored away.

That year, the kids received so many toys that opening presents was a new process of "rip this box open, see what it is and toss it aside to go to the next."

It was *obvious* we screwed up. So, we grabbed half the toys and stuck them in the closet to hand back out months later because they were overwhelmed with too many toys. I think this cheapened the holiday and it *never* happened again.

Some things change, some things stay the same.

The younger two (18-year olds) eye those boxes under the tree and you can see them vibrate with pent-up desire to pick up the gifts and shake them. But, they are older now and should show reserve. Personally, I believe they probably DID test them out when we were away.

So much for growing older ;-)

I enjoy the season. But I'm ready for a simpler Christmas where we have small amounts of gifts, keeping it more personal and unassuming. I suspect what I want is a small break were I can just enjoy the season without all of the stuff that goes with it.

And we have.

It isn't here yet, but I hope that by the time the little rugrats (AKA grandchildren) are running around my kneecaps, I'll have dispensed with the desire for simpler a Christmas and be ready to spoil the hell out of the kids.

And then send them back with their parents and wave from the doorway, smiling to them as I have a glint in my eyes.

Knowing that the little tool-kit I sent home with the mischievous grandchild will give me new stories to tell in the Author Notes of future books.

Like maybe how the grandchild used the toolkit to take apart the coffee table or something. That shit would be funny as hell!

I know a few men reading this right now are chuckling. A few of my lady fans are shaking their heads at me, knowing that I will do this.

Damn right I'll do this.

I have twenty-five years to pent up revenge to provide my three boys. And now I'm doubly dangerous because I have fans I can ask for SUGGESTIONS! So, if you happen to care to add to YOUR review what you might do to 'give the spirit of Christmas (or enter other holiday here)' for your grandchildren join me.

We might as well all get in trouble with our spouses.

I hope you enjoy your holiday, your 2018 and the rest of the years. We have been blessed with you reading and interacting with our stories and I hope YOU have enjoyed them as much as we enjoy writing them for you.

Happy Holidays!
Michael

BOOKS BY CANDY CRUM

TALES OF THE FEISTY DRUID

with Michael Anderle

The Arcadian Druid (01) - The Undying Illusionist (02) - The Frozen
Wasteland (03) - The Deceiver (04) - The Lost (05) - The Damned (06)
Into The Maelstrom (07)

THE THERIAN CHRONICLES

with Amanda Browning

The Dark Professor (1) The Therian Prince (2)

To see ALL of Candy's different books check out her website below

Website:
http://www.candycrumbooks.com

Facebook
https://www.facebook.com/groups/thecandyshopgroup/

Michael Anderle Social

Website:
http://www.lmbpn.com

Email List:
http://lmbpn.com/email/